Copyright © 2023 Onaje Barbee

Library of Congress Control Number: 2023923592

ISBN: 979-8-9897382-0-5

Printed In the United States of America

First Edition

Onaje Barbee

Planet Zoo Entertainment

5 STAR GENERAL

VOL. 2
Street Marine

By
ONAJE 'GANGSTA BOI' BARBEE

Table of Contents

DEDICATION

FIRST & FOREMOST: G.O.D., Thank You for allowing me to make it out of the eye of the storm. For being down for me when I wasn't down for myself. Lifting me when I couldn't hold my head. Carrying me through all the struggles that would break the average person. Wiping tears from my eyes, breathing life into my soul. Giving me encouragement and strength when I was broken mentally. Whenever I lost focus, you would make it straightforward for me.

Thank you for allowing me to make it to an age where I can reflect on how much you always held my hand and carried me. You kept me safe as a boy in a world where only the strong could survive. In a world where I could've lost easily, you put me in the presence of the righteous. The people who would nurture me instead of abusing me. Allowing me to be raised by the wolves so I could be prepared for the world I lived in. Helped me to choose mostly right when I could quickly choose left.

For helping me maintain my mind through all the losses I would endure. Giving me hope to cope and the will to win and never give up. I love you more than words could ever say or express. Thank you! Please give anybody who reads these pages the love and support you have shown me.

SECONDLY, MY BEAUTIFUL WIFE(PRETTY): Thank you for riding the wave of the most complex human being on earth. Again, G.O.D. gave me the best by bringing our union together. My personalities and ways would break the average. You're above and beyond the standard, so I Love You more than any other woman! You can have my rib, lung, heart, and last breath. Thank you for dealing with all the trauma, pain, and hurt that comes with me. We go through problems, but I'm happy as long as we go through them together. Thank you for bringing the four most influential people into existence. Thank you for All the sacrifices you have made for our lives to stay united. When you hurt, I hurt. When you smile, I smile. No matter our struggles, you are still the prettiest girl on earth to me. I Love You Always! Thank You for being perfectly imperfect.

TO ONAJE JR, GINO, TE'DASHII, & JE'RAH (LIL PRETTY) Barbee: I have been trying to have you all since I was a teenager. God wouldn't allow it to happen on my time but on his. I now know why. I wasn't ready, and he knew I would not be the best version of myself for you to have someone to look to as the standard reflection of a man's appearance.

Thankfully, he brought you and your mother to me when the timing was right. You are all better than me in every way.

Every time I look at you, my heart jumps for joy. You'll give me the reasons needed for me to step up to levels I couldn't have imagined. Because of you, I'm afraid to fail, lose, and not do my best at everything.

You'll be more than extraordinary. The bond that we have is something I've yearned for all of my life. You'll provide me with the best things on earth. Happiness, joy, peace, balance, stability, strength, encouragement, love, understanding. I can go on forever with words attempting to describe how you'll make me feel every second of every minute of every hour of every day. I love you to the moon and back. Whatever you go through, you should know you will always have me in your corner to help see it through.

MY EXTENDED FAMILY: The Crawford's, The Hammond's, The Anderson's, The Crooms, The Barbee's, The Conley's, The Riley's Thank You for being there when most needed growing up and now. I have learned something from all of you. The stuff taught helps me give my family the best things in life because of what I learned from you. May we continue to grow our bond to last the test of time.

PLANET ZOO ENTERTAINMENT LLC: Mr. Wayne Daniels, you're more than a business partner to me. More than a friend, comrade, or associate. More like a brother. We have known each other for more than three decades. You're the epitome of a King. It is more than an honor to be in business with you. With you, I know the world is at our fingertips.

All our dreams, wishes, and goals will be accomplished with you at the helm. Thank You for dealing with my bull crap and not allowing my setbacks never to set us back. With you and I coming together to be one, the world shakes with intimidation. May G.O.D. continue to bless P.Z.E., you, yours, and everything we attempt.

Thank You to everyone who does business with us. B. Mitchell, Lil Knoc, Adonis DAHOTTEST, Don Elway, King Slumpz, and the rest. May our bonds last a lifetime.

To The Community Of SKYLINE: you're more than a community to me. More than a neighborhood. Because of that environment, I grew to be more than a man. More than a soldier. You have given me tools that I continue to use today and hand down to my seeds so they can be the best. I was taught discipline like the military. We have suffered losses, setbacks, and carnage, yet we still overcome all. You're my first love. My forever love.

I yearn to see you thrive and be better than me and ours. When I think about you, my heart leaps. For the love of you, I went hard in the paint. I put my life on the line more than a few times more than a few ways. You raised me never to bow down and bow out. I learned how to endure struggles with my head held high at all times. Walk with my chest out. Be strong regardless of situations. Through Pop Warner football, I was broken down and built up to be the best version of myself. Friendships with the best kind of humans on earth.

Taught me how to ride a skateboard, a bike, and pop a willy. Taught me how to play baseball, football, soccer, and basketball. Taught me sex education. Taught me how to get at a girl. I lived with you so much that I even lost my virginity at Skyline Park. When I think of you, only the best thoughts flood my mind. I Thank G.O.D. for raising me in this environment. From the TOPS to the Bottoms. Everything around and within. The entire East side. No matter where I'm in this world, you are with me. To all Soldiers lost. The ones before me, the ones I knew, and the ones I didn't. Thank you for your commitment and service; you shall live through us all.

To my OG Kenneth' Tank Bo-Bo' Anderson: Thank You for being the epitome of what a Real O.G. looks like and behaves regardless of obstacles one may face. Because of you, I learned how to be an O.G.

To All The Dead Homies from San Diego & Abroad: R.I.P. Gino' 'Lunatick' Langston, Billy' Ck-Bill" Matthis, Jason" Baby-Skyline" Riley, Ronald "Ron BO" Rush Jerome "SUPE" Brunson Jabari Anderson, Kenneth Hammond, Troy 'Buddy' Anderson

James Willis Barbee Jr. 'Pops' Who gave me all the G.A.M.E. when you didn't have money. My best friend who I could talk to about inner most feelings. Who always gave me the best answer. Which was for me to talk to GOD. Who helped me to find the light in the darkness. Thank You for the wisdom, knowledge, and understandings. You always said I wouldn't understand how you felt about me until I had kids. Now that I do I comprehend what you meant. Much Love.

Chapter 1

Jackers & Flockers

Before I begin. I want to tell law enforcement agencies that this book is my fantasy. Some stories may be similar to crimes committed in the past and present. However, this is fictional.

E-40 and The Click came through the speakers as we took the fastest route to Freeway 94 eastbound. Once we hit the freeway, the music went into knock status, pumping me up. I missed the city of San Diego, but I was back!

I had reached the next level with the C.K. Riders—I felt like a boss with the cocked MAC-10 on my lap, feeling the power in my hands as I held it, knowing I was ready to shoot. I was wrath, and I was coming. I never thought about going to jail; the only thought in my mind was the hope I'd get to shoot tonight. But we weren't looking for trouble because we were in a registered vehicle, and that wasn't how the C.K. Riders got down.

We had to roll through the enemy's turf to get to our set. My thoughts were of busting. I gripped the trigger tighter as we swerved through the streets of South East San Diego.

We exited the freeway in the community of Emerald Hills. Instantly, the radio turned down. I looked my mentor in the eyes and said, What's up? With a stern look and nod of the head, approval was given.

I knew how he got down because he'd been my teacher; he stared back at me and said, "If any of these dudes are hanging outside, spray them up, and we're going to keep it moving."

There was no noise in the car now—it was quiet, and you could hear a mouse piss on cotton. As we hit corners, we were scanning. Nobody was hanging around. I was mad on the inside because that would have been a bomb reintroduction into San Diego.

Rolling my window up, I leaned back in my seat. I hoped to see anything outside the norm as we drove through Encanto, taking the back streets until we came into the East side of Skyline. Encanto is police central. We moved through 69th Street, creeping through the bottoms, behind the police station alley, and crossing Gribble Street to Skyline Drive. Hit a few more corners to the big home girl's house. This home girl's house was the hangout for the Real Ones.

Before we pulled up and parked, CK Bill, lying in the car's trunk, started rapping a freestyle to the beat on the radio.

CK Bill said, "Gangsta Boi, I hear you got the freestyle Piru, bust one."

"Nah, not me," was my response. I could bust a freestyle, but not now and not tonight. I wanted to see who was what.

It was the more O.G. homies mixing and moving through the house. The big homie on the grill. The music was bumping, alcohol was flowing, and drugs were present. P.C.P. is a favorite among my turf; you could smell the Gorilla Piss as it was being smoked. The C.K. Riders I was with said NO to drugs and barely had alcohol. They were disciplined because of the business we were in—keeping the set safe from outsiders coming through disrespecting and going outward to take care of things ourselves. To do so, We stayed ready so we didn't have to *get* prepared.

I had the MAC-10 on me, and I felt it necessary to stay in position from the back to the front. While I was in the back sipping liquor, the O.G. told me about the last time they were hanging here at the homegirl spot where the police gang unit came through. One of the homies got caught in the attic. With that story, I was ready to leave. Before hearing that, it was nothing, but getting violated and sent back to C.Y.A.—and not getting sex—from hanging over here was a deal breaker for me.

I was ready to bounce, but I was still having a good time; the homeboys and home girls were showing love with laughter, food, and music.

Then I thought I would instead post in the front yard for a running chance if needed. I knew where I was on the turf, so I could hit a couple of fences and be good to move around.

About half a second later, A loud commotion. The big homie and my mentor got into it. The big homie wanted to use my mentor's pistol. My mentor said I told you I had one for you. Come through and get it. Then it clicked in my mentor's brain that the big homie wanted him to come and find him to let him borrow his pistol. That's when it got turned up a notch, and things started to spiral out of control.

The big homie jumped inside his car like he was going for his banger. My mentor tapped me, and I pulled out the gun and gave it to him. He waved it toward the big homie. The big homie got out of his car quickly. From that point, they started arguing. It was time to catch the fade between my mentor and the big homie. No pistols were allowed; two big homies went, along with my mentor and his right hand. I tried to jump in the car with my mentor and the two homies that would catch the fade. One was to fight, and the other was there to watch his back. But I was told I couldn't roll because I had the MAC-10 on me.

This was my first night out, and it was significantly active. I loved it and thought, *This was one hell of a night.*

The homies came flying back, still talking mess about what had transpired. This turned into big homies versus young homies in the set, and the war lasted about a month. Nobody got shot. The big homies didn't want to relinquish the turf. It was one of the times when many of my elders were out simultaneously, and they felt like they were young again. They knew they weren't doing any major stuff but thought we weren't showing enough love towards them. We didn't care about how they felt. This was our turf now, and we were doing all the work around here and around town. It was time for them to bow out and down to something more significant than themselves. Since they were not understanding, we would show them what was up.

The spot got too hot at the home girl's house, so me and the two homies left. We rolled silently, all in deep thought, to my mother's house, where they dropped me off. Of course, I was thinking about getting me some sex with my Elementary School Kid. At my earliest convenience, I would make my way to Caramel and my E.S.K.

I got out and tossed the P to my mentor. He said, "Welcome home, Skyline," before we shook hands, and he pulled me in close for a hug. He whispered, "You see what you come home to?" War.

I looked at him and said, "You know what's up."

As I strolled off towards the front door to my mother's house, he said, "Make sure you do enough sex for the both of us." He smiled at me, then hopped in his car and sped off.

I knocked on the door, and my mother opened it. I said, "Hey, Mom." I entered the house slightly tipsy. I was utterly oblivious to her attitude. It was one morning, and I just wanted to stay up twenty-four hours. My sisters were still up and were happy to see me. My mother, of course, had a stank attitude by the time I got there, probably taking offense to me not coming straight home with them, not understanding that I was fresh out and didn't want to go straight home to do nothing. I didn't know if it was me or her being selfish.

So, the tension between her and me grew, and I knew staying there wouldn't last long. My mother and I had been having a disconnect since I was born. Now that I was becoming the gangster she helped to create, I was too much for her. I could tell she didn't like my attitude right out of the gate, but I didn't care. She picked her battles. On my first day out, she let it slide. Trust, she saved the argument for another day.

My sister gave me some movies that came out while I was down. I stayed up, watching all the movies, then fell asleep. I woke up the next day knowing what we had to do: Go and meet my parole officer and get all my requirements to stay on the streets.

Early the following day. My mother and sisters got into her car with me and headed towards my parole office. We got off the freeway in Mission Valley, walked into a building on the left, and got on the elevator to the third floor. Then, we sat in the waiting room for my parole officer. After about five minutes, a lady called us to the back. My mother and sisters stayed in the waiting area.

I took a seat immediately, and we began with the main issue: gang affiliation. I was not to have any contact with known gang members, whether they had been to jail or not. In my neighborhood, the police put everybody on gang documentation. I was to not be in or around Skyline, from the Bottoms to the Tops. They wanted me to go around if able. I would be drug tested every month. I was to go to school and find a job. I had other terms and conditions, which pretty much summed up.

I took the paperwork, went back to my mom and sisters, and we left.

Once we got into the car, my mom asked where I wanted to go. I told her to take me to my grandmother's house in 69. When we arrived, I told my mom I would be home later. She asked if I would enroll in school. I said I'd check out a few today.

I entered my grandmother's house and was greeted with a familiar scene. My grandmother was sitting down in the kitchen. Bear, our family dog, had been poisoned and been dead for quite a while now. My father was sleeping in the garage; he wouldn't be up until late afternoon.

I yelled, "Pop! Pop! Get up! Get up!"

Then I heard him yell out, "Ok!"

aunt Sandy Barbee, aunt Sis, and Queen P wasn't there. I asked my grandmother, "Where my relatives were at?"

Lil Bad News was in jail. Trigger Happy was at my Uncle A's house in Encanto. Gino "Lunatick" Langston was in a group home called The House of Hope in Lil Africa Piru turf.

I asked my Dad to drive me to Uncle A's house just as a little girl walked out of the back room. I said, "Who is that?"

"Queen P's daughter," my grandmother said.

"What?" I immediately noticed her arm was messed up. "What happened?"

An accident in Arizona messed them up. "Damn."

With that, my father came out of the garage and said, "Come on." If he was happy I was out, I couldn't tell.

We jumped into my grandmother's car, drove down the hill, and stopped at the light. Made a left and went to Imperial, made a right, a left, and another right, then drove up the hill to Trigger Happy house is at the top of the mountain on a dead end.

My relative Trigger Happy greeted me with the P handshake and a forty-ounce beer. He pulled me in for a hug and whispered, "We got straps."

I pulled back and gave him a devilish grin. I asked, "What's up, relative?

My pop nodded his head to us, saying bye. I nodded back.

It felt good to see him. It had been a long time since I saw him last. I left him in Campo when I got kicked out. The Bloods and Crips riot we were in together when I got kicked out. Since then, he has been back in jail. He went to a C.Y.A. alternative in Nevada called R.O.P. (Rites of Passage) and hadn't been out long before me.

We walked into Uncle A's house, who had not been there since he had a job working for the city. My Uncle's girlfriend was there with a couple of my Trigger Happy's little crew. I knew them all from one time or another from hanging out. I shook hands before taking a seat on the couch. My Uncle's girlfriend was rolling weed in blunts on the table. At this time, I had never encountered a blunt. My relative offered me some alcohol. I declined. Offered the blunt. I declined. I never liked beer or weed, so I passed on both.

My gangster-ism was at the forefront, so I paid attention to my surroundings, checking out their location and company. There was a Crip there, and I didn't like that he was hanging with them. Yes, I knew him. Set Trip and Rider, their Dad's side of the family, are mostly Crips, and this was their friend. Still, he had no place hanging and banging with us. Watching and spying on our movements.

Before, my Uncle would barely allow us to come by, let alone hang out. He usually was with his crew of beastly Samoans—besides my relative Lil Bad News, we couldn't hang. Lil Bad News was revered as a gangster by my entire family, except for my father. He was treated as the golden goose.

Trigger Happy signaled with his eyes for me to come over to him. We walked down some stairs into another room, where he opened the closet: an artillery of arsenal. I smiled. Then, he lifted the bed. More guns; my smile got bigger. Then he took me out of the house to a garage in the back, where one of the dudes lived. More guns. I thought to myself, *It's on.*

I felt good about being home now. That day, I hung out with my relative and checked out his operation—not talking much but listening, watching, and peeping the game of our new environment—planning, plotting, and strategizing.

Trigger Happy, his homies, and I strolled to the liquor store for a few things. While walking back to the house, we stopped at

The Pinkies apartment complex, and Trigger Happy said, "This is ours."

We went to apartment after apartment. They were drinking, smoking, getting plates of food, and kissing all the girls. Gino "Lunatick" Langston called from the group home, and someone handed me the phone. Hearing his voice felt good; I hadn't talked to him in a long time. He was my baby brother in my heart, not by blood, and I kept him with me as much as possible, giving him all I could: money, time, knowledge, love, and game—the good, the bad, and the ugly.

When we returned to Uncle A's house, it was dark, and he was off work. I wanted to see what he was doing now and was very interested to hear his thoughts. To this point, he and I didn't have the best relationship. I was wondering how he would treat me now. I was older and fresh out of C.Y.A. (California Youth Authority)—that place was on a different level. After serving time, I understood why. Now, I wanted to see if it would influence our relationship in one way or another.

As soon as I saw him, he was full of alcohol. I asked him if he was drinking before he got off work. He started talking crap—but in a good way—and pulling me in like family. That caught me off guard, but I was surprised by how much he had changed in the few years I was away. Years earlier, he put on this super gangster image, and now he was drinking, smoking sherm, and active with the young, telling jokes and being the life of the party. My Uncle still had a gangster persona but was not as standoffish as he once was. Something had changed. What? Who? How, I did not know. I didn't care. I could be cool with this person. Plus, I need the heat.

I was glad he opened his arms and pulled me in. It took a long time for this to happen, but it wasn't too late. I then let the hatred slide down my back as I started to overcome the petty differences between us. I hung out for as long as possible, soaking up this new location. The Shack was a thing of the past—the homie's mom sold the house. Although my Uncle's house was not running like The Shack, it was where the homies would hang. Now and then, the older homies would pull up and hang out.

After a long while, I called my pops to come and get me to take me to my mother's house.

Chapter 2

'Got It on Me'

The next day, I would start looking for a school to attend. My Dad came and got me, and I asked him to take me to Caramel's house in Skyline first. I still hadn't called her or found my Elementary School Kid. I wanted to pop up on them. It was dark now, but not too late for me to go to her house and get cussed out by her mom.

I walked to her doorway, my heart beating through my chest. I was eager to see her but hoped my dream wasn't true. I rang the doorbell, and I could hear it throughout the house.

"Who is it?" a soft-spoken female asked from behind the door.

I said, "Onaje." Slowly, she unlocked the door and opened it, exposing only her head. It was Caramel.

She didn't ask me to come in, but I stepped inside anyway. It was dark, and I couldn't see very far inside from where we were standing. I walked into the living room to the left and turned around. I saw her from the back as she closed the door.

Then she turned around and said, "I'm pregnant."

Immediately, my heart sank to my knees. I didn't know what to do as she started apologizing about the pregnancy.

I turned sour and asked, scowling, "How far along are you?" knowing full well that she was way past the point of no return. Still, I had to ask. I was hoping for the best. But she said she would be giving birth soon.

I became distant and looked at her like she was an enemy. She began crying. Because of this, I started saying anything that came to mind, anything I thought would cut and hurt her deeply. She cried more. She suggested that we run away together, that it wasn't too late for us and our relationship.

I said coldly, "It's over." I did, however, feel some retribution through her tears. Still, I knew that she and I would never be. She tried to come in for a hug, and I threw her arms down in refusal.

"I'm out of here," I said, opening the door and leaving without another word.

I jumped in the car with my Dad and left. While at my Dad's side of the family for the day, I found a way to contact my Elementary School Kid. From her letters, I discovered she lived near my mother's house. My pops and I didn't talk about much on the way to my mom's. My mother's house never gave me a good feeling, although that was where I would rather be now.

The chances of me being violated were high. Because of this, I believed my mother and I tolerated each other for as long as we could.

When I got to my mom's, I watched movies until I fell asleep. Again. I wasn't even thinking about my mom's side of the family and didn't allow them to see me. I knew I hadn't changed in the ways they hoped. I wasn't thinking about changing; by this point, my mother and sisters knew.

I woke up early the next day, knowing what I had to get done. I had to find a continuation school with a woman teacher with whom I might have some action. I wanted the action where I could maneuver and make some things happen regarding graduating. This was the first time I got out of jail and didn't have a girl to have sex with immediately. I would have to start over by finding some girls, and I might as well start here.

My mom went to the garage and started warming up the car. My clothes game was awful. After two years and nine months, my clothes were either gone or no good. My shoes were my God brother's, whose feet were smaller than mine. It was all I had, so I would put it together until I could make some other stuff happen. The good thing was that there were a lot of pairs, so I could find one that matched what I was wearing. After five minutes, I was in my zone, and my mother and I left.

First, I attended the continuation school on Federal Blvd. and Euclid Ave. They had a short Black female teacher who was in her late forties or early fifties and overweight. Undesirable for me, I told my mother after a few seconds in the room, "Let's go. Too many enemies." Surprisingly, I didn't see any known faces that might recognize me. I told her it wouldn't work out, and we left.

Then we went to Lemon Grove Summit and checked on a continuation that I went to before. It was close to my father's house and my side of town. They had a male teacher, and I didn't want that, so we left in a matter of seconds. My mother didn't understand why, so I gave her some flimsy excuse.

We made our way to Spring Valley Summit, the first continuation school I attended after leaving Campo in 1993. When I arrived, Mr. Six was there, and it felt good to see him. Some of my homies were there, but going there was my last option. So we shared a few laughs, and I left.

As far as I knew, we'd been through all the local continuation schools.

My mom asked, "What are you going to do?"

"I have a couple of other schools in mind," I said. "First, I must get the addresses because I don't know where they are."

"Do you want to go to your dad's house?" she asked.

I told her, "No, not today. I want to go home to relax." I could tell this was what she wanted to hear; she and my sisters got a kick from me slowing down.

I relaxed for more than a few hours to appreciate them, enough time for some of my relatives to visit. My relative, Jabari Anderson, came to see me during this time. On my mother's side of the family, he was the one I was closest to. He was a year older than me, and through my desire to be more of an active gangster from my turf, we drifted apart. He was brown-skinned, about my height, with a long beard down to his chest. Even though he looked different since the last time I saw him, we still had a good time. We laughed and kicked it for a while, and then he left.

After hanging around and seeing my relatives, I figured it would be an excellent time to go to my Elementary School Kid's house. So I told my mother I would stroll to a friend's house and return later. It just so happened my Elementary School Kid's place was down the street and around the corner.

When I arrived, I saw her relatives, my homies whom I met her through, were there. We talked, we laughed, and we got caught up. It was good to see those guys. They were my extended brothers, and like freedom, I had missed them much. Since I got kicked out of camp, I hadn't seen or heard from her relative, Ol' Boi. Her mother always talked a lot of crap to me, but it was good to see her all the same. I spoke with her quite a few times while incarcerated.

While they were drinking and smoking, a phone call came through from my Elementary School Kid. She didn't know that I was out yet. I grabbed the phone, full of excitement.

"Hello?" I said in a calm, smooth voice.

"Who is this?" she asked, and it sounded sexy as hell.

"Who do you want it to be?"

I could tell by the smile in her voice that she knew who it was. She said, "Onaje, when did you get out?"

"A few days ago," I said. "Where you at?"

She said, "School."

"What school do you go to?"

"A continuation school on Paradise Valley Rd. Called Worthington Summit," she said. I didn't know they had a continuation school there. "When can I see you?"

"When you want to see me."

"Today. Now," she said.

"I don't have a car," I answered.

She began to talk about some guys that wanted to get her after school. Then she asked me to give the phone to her relative. So I gave the phone to Ol' Boi, and he listened to the details. After that, I began being nosy, trying to hear the conversation. She got into it with some of my homies, and they wanted to get her after school. I had never hung out with them, so it was none of my business, but she wanted us to come to the school.

The only question that Ol' Boi asked was, "How are we supposed to get there?" The next thing I heard was, "OK."

He gave the phone back to me, and I said, "You stay in some crap."

Without giving me the info, she asked if I would come with them. Of course, I said yes. I was horny as hell.

"The ride is on its way," she said, and a few moments later, a guy pulled up in a long, beat-up Cadillac. He was brown-skinned, more towards light than brown. Judging by his appearance, he was older than me.

He said, "What's up," to her folks while eyeing me as I observed him. Then, he walked straight into the house and began talking to her mother. I didn't pay any mind, really, and after a few minutes, he reappeared and asked them if they were ready to leave.

"Is he going?" he asked the others, talking about me. They said yes, and we piled into his car.

During the ride, they introduced us. We got there before school was out, so we hung around the school area in a strip mall. It was during this time Ol' Boi told me who the guy was. He said that he was the Elementary School Kid's boyfriend. I didn't care much. I knew she had somebody because she was too fine not to.

Before they let the class out, I walked inside to see what it looked like. Plus, I wanted her reaction to seeing me after all these years without her dude-hating. Her response was exactly what I was looking for. I tried to strip her sexy ass down right there and give it to her.

After getting the reaction I wanted, I was now looking at the school since I needed to find a place to attend. This school would be perfect; it was near my community and everything else I needed. When I walked in, I encountered not one female teacher in her twenties but two of them: one White and one Black. I couldn't believe it. From the looks of it, my wish might become a reality. One was at the chalkboard while one was sitting in a chair in the office. I looked around the class to see the female population besides my Elementary School Kid, and there were plenty. From a glance, it appeared to be more females than guys. All doable. I just wanted to be around pussy. Stepping out of class, I backed up to see her dude and catch their reactions. I was sure she would put on a show; that's how she was. She would try any guy because it's in her D.N.A.

The guys who were supposed to come up to get her didn't show. The teachers were also feeling themselves, so they came outside momentarily. I was able to size them up enough to know that I would be attending this school.

We piled inside the dude's car. I sat in the back seat. The next thing I knew, an elementary school kid had climbed in with me and sat on my lap. Because there were so many people in the car, other people were in the front seat with him. He drove off like that.

After about half a mile, it sunk in that he was tripping. He pulled over and told her to get in the front, then started ranting and raving about what she was doing. She calmly said that there were no seats. He talked his crap, but it was nothing to her. Her relatives laughed hysterically because they knew the get down. He swerved through the lane, flying through traffic while making his way back to her mother's house. I know he wanted to get her and me away from each other. I could feel his eyes staring at me in the rear-view mirror. I watched him with a mean mug, knowing I wouldn't get any time with her today.

He and the Elementary School Kid left fast once we returned to her mother's house. Her relatives and I kicked it into the night, telling war stories and cracking jokes. They told me about the dude Elementary School Kid was with, what he had going on, and that he had her mom wrapped around his finger. He had a hustle and was giving her stacks of money and gifts. Immediately, I noticed her attitude, which had always been shady, but there was something different about it this time. Now I knew exactly why. I was a threat to the program that they had going on, but it was all good. She still had love for me because I was like family. However, she would try to keep me and her daughter separated.

After getting caught up with my family, I had to make a move. Laying down on my bed, I reflected on the day. A piece of my puzzle had come together, and I knew I would go to that school and apply the next day. I didn't like the fact that getting some sex was null and void. It would be something that I just had to get over. I was seventeen and would be eighteen in five months, but my mother still had control issues with me. I could tell she had something to say, but she bit her tongue for now. I was thankful for that. However, I did feel that the inevitable would be coming soon. I thought it best to start getting my ducks in a row for when that day came.

I hadn't been back to my turf since my first day out. I hit and missed. I also knew my chances of getting violated went from zero to one hundred, and I didn't get any sex yet. I did feel like I could do me and beat the system. The set was active, and I was on the enthusiastic crew. I knew what came with me hanging out. It would be nothing to find myself in some Rider activity. I had it on the menu.

After watching more movies with my sister, I was on my way to sleep. My mother walked into the room and gave me the phone. It was Elementary School Kid, and she said that she ditched her dude. She said she was coming through if I wanted her to.

I said, "I was on my way to sleep, but I'll get up for you."

About twenty minutes later, she came through looking and smelling good. We went into my bedroom and sat on the bed. She began running down the relationship with the dude, telling me the basics. I wanted to know who and what type of individual I was dealing with to understand how to play the situation.

Once we got the ins and outs, we got into what she came for. It had been some time since we had sexed last, and she wanted to show me the updated version. Immediately she took my penis out and began giving me some of the best heads I ever had. She looked right at me, pulling my penis in and out of her mouth, spitting on it like a professional, and massaging my balls with her other hand. Then she went down and put my balls in her mouth. It felt so good my knees buckled, and I had to get a hold of the bed to balance myself.

After about ten minutes of wooing me with her bomb head game, we got into bed. I could feel the wetness of her vagina just as soon as I put my hand on her crotch. I slipped a finger in. It was wet and tight. No wonder she was playing the sucker like a sucker; he wasn't doing any damage to her. We couldn't do it like we wanted because we were in a bunk bed—she couldn't ride on top of me, and I couldn't beat it up the way I liked. I don't know why we didn't do it on the floor.

We had some excellent intense sex for twenty minutes, and I was ready to cum. I wanted to get her pregnant. I told her, "I'm leaving this penis inside your vagina," and then came inside her with everything I had.

She said she couldn't get pregnant because she was on some shot. I didn't want to have sex with her no more. Pointless.

However, after five minutes, I was ready for round two. I began by putting my finger in her warm, wet vagina. I wanted to taste it, so I parted her legs and slipped my tongue inside her. She tasted good. I nibbled and sucked on her clit, licking it, pulling on it, and biting it ever so gently. She was feeling it and started humping me back, lifting her ass off the bed and pushing herself into my mouth. She grabbed the back of my head, and I got aggressive, slipping some fingers inside her. She was so wet, and my penis was so hard. I missed her vagina. I couldn't control the way I was eating her vagina—I was totally out of my mind, sucking on it with my entire being.

After I got her cum inside my mouth, I slid my penis into her tight, juicy vagina. There was no making love this round. We were sexing. I was trying to hump her brains out, but because we were at my mother's house with my sisters, we couldn't yell and let out what was going on inside us; we contained the savage beast within out of respect for the others in the house. I put her legs on my shoulder and pounded into her, kissing her neck and biting her ear. She loved it rough and rugged, and I knew it.

It was late into the early morning hours when we got done. She left, and I went to sleep feeling great.

Chapter 3

'Outside'

I woke up the next day with the thought of applying to that summit first thing. That school had two shifts, one in the day and one in the afternoon. The morning shift had a different teacher. I didn't know if it was a man or a woman and didn't care because I had seen what I wanted and felt good about the percentages of knocking one of them.

That afternoon, I went to the school and inquired about enrolling. The White lady was the one I was talking with. She looked to me to be in her mid-to-late-twenties. She was gorgeous, tall, and had a nice body with a beautiful personality. I didn't know if she was putting on some act. First, she said they needed to get my school records, give them my parole officer's number, contact my parole officer, and give them their information. That would get the ball rolling.

Then, she asked, "Do you want the morning or afternoon class?"

I said, "I'd prefer the afternoon class. What time do I have to be there? What time do we get out?"

"Class starts at twelve p.m.," she answered, "and ends at four."

"That's cool," I said. "I'm no early bird."

After attempting to check her out to the best of my ability, I put on my best smile and told her I would contact my parole officer ASAP.

"Where did you parole from?" she asked, and I knew I would get some reaction once I told her.

"C.Y.A."

"You were in C.Y.A.?" she said. "How long were you in there?" When I told her, she was in disbelief; I could tell by the look on her face. Then, she asked, "Are you under eighteen?"

"Yes."

I could tell what she was thinking—I didn't look like a hardened criminal doing that kind of time. The good thing about doing time was that it preserved my youth. Besides that, I didn't think my presence ever gave off the vibe of a real-life gangster.

With that, in the most gangster way I could muster, I said I would get at her later when I got my stuff in order and walked out. As soon as I left, I felt confident about getting some action.

I jumped in my mom's car and asked her to take me to my Dad's house. It was time for me to return to the turf and see what was happening there. My other best friends on the turf from before C.Y.A. had moved down south. Around the Nine, things had gotten slow; you had to be down near the dungeon to be around some fun activities. The dungeon is where my homie Tink lived. It was a cramped little space in the basement of his house, right next to the liquor store—a prime spot to catch up with homies and girls. Also, it was an excellent way to flag people down because so much traffic ran up and down Imperial Avenue.

The Pinkies was another good spot across the street from the dungeon. We used to hang with my little relative's family every now and then, who stayed on the same street as my G'mom just across the train tracks. We grew up with them because of my little relatives' mother and Aunt Sandy, who both dated men there. They had a big family with members from everywhere. Most of their family thought they were CRIPS, the girls and the boys, but they also had some from my turf. We used to do a lot of gambling and swapping stolen items with each other. A lot had happened since I had been down, and we didn't kick it anymore.

To get started on meeting girls fast, I would need some help from my relative, Trigger Happy. He had been out for a while and had several females to talk to. He was a pretty boy, so he always had the hook up in that department. Besides that, he could help me catch up with some of my past girls; I wanted to get some more sex. Even though he liked to get faded from the morning into the night, he still kept up with everyone and everything.

While hanging out, I asked him, "Do you know where any of the girls I used to have sex with are?"

He said, "Hoe Bear, stay by the trolley station." The trolley station was right down the street. "At night, sometimes the homies are over there."

"Cool," I said. "Well, tonight, we're going through."

"She'll be over there with her baby daddy," he said. But I didn't care; I was looking for more sexual healing. "Till then," he said, "let's go around the corner to the Pinkies." He always hung with a bunch of dudes that rode on his balls. He liked that stuff, which was fantastic. I wasn't tripping; I didn't particularly appreciate hanging with many dudes and no girls.

So we walked to the Pinkies to one of his soon-to-be girlfriends' houses. Her name is Krafty. She kept different types of traffic coming through her spot. At the time, she was dating another one of our homies. Supposedly, she had just had a baby with him. She stayed on the top floor so we could see everything happening. While hanging over there, I liked that there was always a bunch of girls coming and going out of different holes. I would find myself drifting in and out of the apartment, trying to see what was happening in the area: if any rivals were sneaking in and out, if the police were constantly creeping through, or if a bunch of girls were going and coming.

After all that time, I noticed I wasn't running up on girls like I once had. I was a lot more quiet, observant, and paranoid. I noticed that Krafty, and her friends were watching me, probably tripping off me because I wasn't on the same page as my little relative and his friends. She had a bunch of home girls coming and leaving her apartment. My relative said her mom was always at work, so her house was the spot. She was about fifteen and had already had two kids. Both of the kids had two daddies. She was having some severe sex. She didn't have a body, but she did have a cute face with the personality of a Queen.

The music stayed blasting, but it was always that Mary J. Blige song from the soundtrack *Waiting To Exhale,* "Not Gon Cry." I was not too fond of that slow stuff. My relative Trigger Happy was right there with Special, loving that music. After so much of that, I was ready to go.

I said, "You ready to show me where Hoe Bear lives?" noticeably agitated.

By this time, he was feeling good and faded and said, "Yeah, come on," like a gangster with an attitude. Trigger Happy always knew how to put the extras on, especially if he had an audience. In this case, he had dudes and females around, so anything he said or did was with a statement. Being with him my whole life, I knew the business.

The other homeboy had just got his license and had a car, so he drove us to where she was, about two blocks away, directly across from Trolley Station. I knocked on the door.

She said, "Who is it?"

"G Boi!" I said, and she opened the door with a smile on her face.

"What's up, Onaje?" she asked. "When did you get out?" It sounded like she missed me but didn't invite us in.

"Couple days ago," I said. I tried to look around her to see what I could see. Laying on the couch was some dude. I couldn't see his face, and she made sure of that by blocking herself and the rest of the house with the door.

Just to mess with her, I said, "What's happening? We can't come in or what?"

"Nah, my daddy is here," she said.

"Let us up in there and meet the dude, homegirl," I whispered to her. I hadn't met her dude, but what I did know about him was that he was an older man from our immediate enemy's turf.

My relative took that as a sign and went in. He became loud and belligerent, ensuring the enemy could hear us at the door gang banging.

Like the woman she was, she didn't want her baby daddy to feel uncomfortable and immediately went on the defense. She quickly whispered for me to get in touch with her soon and told me who to get her number from. "I have to go," she said before quickly shutting the door.

With that, we lingered inside her parking garage, still talking loudly, knowing they could hear us even with the television on. We had guns, so we were turned up. Hoe Bear and I had a strange relationship. I took her virginity in seventh grade when she lived around the corner from us and a couple of houses down from the Shack. For the most part, we had grown up with each other. My relatives and I had broken into their home. Once to see what their life was like out of pure boredom. I didn't take anything, but my younger relative wanted their little brother's game system and stole it.

The evening got her virginity was some of the craziest stuff I had been in up to that point. I was hanging on the Nine all day and somehow made my way to her house, hanging with her and her older sister. I wanted to get with her sister, who was also older than me by a year, but she always said no. I didn't have what she liked at all. But now her sister was different. She was more than thick and less than fat but, all the same, a big girl. Dark skinned with short hair and about my height. Hoe Bear went to school with me and was best friends with the girl I was dating, and I'd just taken her virginity a few weeks ago.

After flirting a lot, she and her sister started talking and whimpering back and forth. I was nibbling on her neck and kissing her, whispering sweet nothings in her ear, trying to rub on her sweet spot. She was willing to give me that flower but needed more encouragement. I kissed somewhere on her neck, and her knees buckled. I heard a moan escape her lips.

I said, "Come on, baby, let me get some of that good."

"But you go with my best friend," she said.

"Don't let that stop us. She's not going to know nothing," I said. "This is between me, you, and GOD."

I put my hand on her pants zipper, trying to get it down while kissing her neck gently. Then with my tongue on her skin, I rubbed my hand up and down over her twat. Laying on her mother's bed, we heard a noise, and thinking it might be her mother, we both jumped up quickly to check the situation. I knew I was close, but that sound might have put me back at first base. It would give her too much time to rethink everything.

After she got back to me, she was back to being shy and stand-off-ish, and I thought, *I don't feel like having to do this all over.*

But then her sister asked, "What's up?"

"She thinks it'll hurt," I said, "and now she's scared."

So her older sister stepped in and began talking her into it. Slowly but surely, I saw the walls were starting to come down, and my shot at sexing was going back up. Next thing I know, my penis is nice and hard, and I'm back on her, trying to get to that nectar.

About a half hour later, we were on her mother's bed, and I was licking her neck. Her legs were open, and she was moaning in my ear. Now I got my hands on her sweet spot, moving up and down over the outside of her pants. Still licking and sucking on her neck, I unbuttoned her pants, pulled them down, and threw them aside. I positioned myself between her legs and slid the head of my penis to the entry of her nectar. She grabbed me hard as I slowly tried to get to the back of her pussy. She moaned and groaned, and her pussy was hot and wet; the juices were flowing down the shaft of my dick, but it was still so tight.

After about five minutes of easing it in, my dick was more than halfway inside, and I could tell she was starting to feel it. Her grip loosened, and her groaning subsided. Finally, I was in, and that pussy was feeling good. I was still on her neck, licking, sucking, and biting while humping a little faster now. She still had her arms around me, but now she pulled me closer. There were no more bumps in the road; it was smooth sailing, and we were fucking. She loved it.

"How does that feel?" I asked.

She moaned and said, "It feels so good."

"Your pussy is wet."

"You like it?"

"Hell yeah."

After twenty minutes of good sexing, I wanted to bust a nut. Just like I was taught from watching porn, I pulled out and jerked my penis off until the cum came shooting out unto her pubic hairs.

She had a baby before I went to jail, and I knew the timing was off slightly. Still, I had a possibility, or at least I had hoped, of being her baby's father. During this time, I started to have doubts about me having kids. I began to think this way because, first and foremost, I had been getting a lot of sex. I was barebacking my fair share and knew that someone should have been pregnant by now. And yeah, of the girls whose virginities I got, a couple got pregnant. While in juvenile hall in my second term, I pulled off some moles on my penis. After that, it appeared that no girl was getting pregnant.

I badly desired to have a seed at this point. Maybe it was for the wrong reasons, but I didn't care. I wanted what I wanted, and it wasn't happening. And she was one of the first of many women

I had hoped to have my baby. So when I got the chance to put my suspicion out there, I did, and for a minute, it bounced around her head, but in the end, she stuck to her guns and said nope. I admit that her child looked more like the other dude than me.

We left and returned to Krafty's apartment; by this time, it was getting late. She now had two of her friends over, Chuny Baby and Bubbles. Bubbles liked my relative, and Chuny Baby and I constantly bumped heads. She said that she knew me from her relative who had virginized me. Chuny Baby had some nice juicy titties and was pretty in the face, shorter than me, but didn't have a big ass; mediocre at best.

After being over there for about an hour, I decided to shut it down. My relative and I went to my Uncle's house. I called my father to get me to take me to my mother's house. I didn't want to leave but was trying to play the game right for Mom and me. The tension was so high between us that anything might get her to react out of anger and kick me out before I had my next move ready, and I didn't have any alternatives then. My aunt Sis stayed in Spring Valley, but I hadn't had a chance to make it out there yet.

After my Dad came and got me, we stopped at the store, got me some cigarettes, and went to my mother's house. We talked briefly about school, work, and staying out, and I gave him the typical answers. I don't think my Dad cared about what I had going on. He just wanted to talk so the ride wouldn't be so awkward. He meant well, but he was still smoking crack, which was the main thing on his brain. If not that, then he was thinking of his girlfriend. He would be head over heels for his woman even if they were strawberries and looked like men. A strawberry is a woman who would sell everything she had from her soul to her family for some crack, and this is what he would give all his time and energy to. He would think everybody wanted that pussy—family, friends, and enemies. If he left them alone for five minutes, he believed somebody ran some dick up in them.

Finally, we got to my mom's house, and of course, I didn't stay long. I wanted to stop at the Elementary School Kid's house to see what was happening. But, more than anything, I wanted some more pussy. Her dude could have all of her time. Time was something I wouldn't have a lot of going down the line because I was devoted to something else.

After getting to her house, she wasn't there. But her family was, so I stayed, and we played dominoes and talked. After being there for about an hour, Elementary School Kid came home, and a tornado came with her. It seemed like she was trying to shake him cause he hadn't caught up yet, but they all knew he was en route. But she did bring a friend, who was just as cute.

The house was just calm before, but the tension rose fast. Elementary School Kid was loud and full of hatred towards her dude, screaming at her mom that she wasn't going back with him; forget this and forget that. It was the first time I started paying attention to the entire situation. I guess because I had my own stuff I was dealing with, I never thought about what was happening. I was only seventeen then, and she was younger than me, so she had to be maybe fifteen. If she was sixteen, then she had just turned it. She wasn't staying there; she was staying with the dude. The dude was definitely grown, but I didn't know his age. He had a couple of cars that I had seen him drive in.

She was crying and screaming at her mother about him hitting on her and how crazy and jealous he was. One thing I suspected about her was that she would mess with his head. Mainly, she was only there for one reason: his money. Back then, she was too young to honor what he was probably doing and showing her.

He arrived, and she went down the walkway to greet him. Because I enjoy festivities, I always made sure that I was close to the drama where I could see and hear, so I was in the walkway watching. Just as soon as they came by, she stopped, got up on me, and pulled herself close to me. Her friend kept going; the dude did as well. After realizing how he was looking, he came back and told her to bring herself on. She did. But I wasn't even tripping off her dude; it would have been on if he had stepped. He felt it, and I'm sure he got some information on who I was to her and the family. Now I understood that her mother was selling her daughter to him.

That night, her mom agitated me because of the ensuing drama. Her relatives told me it had been smooth sailing until I returned. Now, it was all chaos, and her mom put me at the root of the problem.

The dude went back to his car and came back with gifts. First, he gave her a brand-new white bomber jacket. Then he gave her mom some money. I don't know how much, but she was on his team. She gave me an attitude that I had never seen.

When they left, she left her jacket and pager and told me to get them before I went home. The coat was able to fit me and looked nice, so I did. I could use the pager, so I took it too. I enjoyed the show, but now it was time to go.

I got home at about twelve, and my mother was giving me an attitude like normal. We would often do this song and dance; after a while, she would poke, and just as soon as she did, I would be gone. I had zero tolerance for her because the love wasn't there. I went into my room, watched some movies, and slept.

Chapter 4

Fried Bologna

A couple of days later, I was able to start attending the continuation school with the two female teachers. I sat in the back so I could see what was going on. I first wanted to see who was in the class since safety was necessary. From my Elementary School Kid's information, there were no enemies there. She was in the class with a couple of her friends. Of course, because she thought I was her man, she would attempt to claim me, and I would allow it up to a certain degree. She didn't know what I was conspiring to do or that she was a part of my plans—girls attract other girls.

Immediately, I could tell that Tasha was digging on me. She was a dark-skinned girl with long hair and a smoking hot body. She walked like her booty was too big for her, but on the low, I would get with her.

She began the conversation with, "So you're the guy she has been writing to that was in C.Y.A.?"

"Yeah," I said.

"It's finally nice to put a face to you," she said. "She has been ranting about you for years."

Our conversation was small initially, but we got more involved each day. I needed to know what was going on with Elementary School Kid, so to have someone on the inside was imperative. After all, I was thinking about having a kid with her. A close friend who looked like she wouldn't mind having some of me would be perfect.

I got her number and, soon enough, started communicating with her. She was perfect; she would let me know everything I needed. I discovered Elementary School Kid was head over heels for another guy in the class before ours. The older guy she was with was entirely about the money, and her mom was pushing a hard line on her because of it. I knew already, but I had no idea how much money we were talking about. It wasn't a minor change; it was big bucks. He was into white-collar crimes. He would spoil my girl, her mother, and her friends.

With all the information she gave me about Elementary School Kid, she quickly became a non-factor and slowly went to the bottom of my list. I never got with Tasha; however, I appreciated all that was told to me.

The class was set up where the teacher's office was to the left just as soon as you walked in, with a chalkboard to the right and the chairs opposite it. There weren't that many people in the class—just about fifteen. I guess the black female teacher would do most of the teaching. The white female teacher would often be inside the office, which had windows with blinds that were usually closed.

My plan was simple: to make a statement about who I was and what I was about without saying a word. I would often be in class just playing it cool and attempting to look as fly as possible. First off, I would have my homies come and get me. On the first day, I had my OG Ken-Den, fresh out and dating my aunt Queen P, come pick me up. When he stepped inside the class, he was swollen with muscles, had long hair, Shirley Temple style, and looked fresh to death, from his shoes to his head.

After looking around and spotting me, he said, "Gangsta Boi, you want something from Kentucky Fried Chicken?" in the same parking lot.

I said, "Yeah," and just as he appeared, he disappeared. His presence alone made everybody in the class respect it because he was an O.G., and you could feel his realness through his stature. I could immediately tell that it had done what I needed it to do: make everyone recognize that I was not a buster and was indeed a real one. In my mind, this made a difference in how the teachers would perceive me.

I did notice, however, that the white teacher took students home or to the bus stop after school. A light bulb went off in my head. One day, when the timing was right, I would utilize that to get to her.

After leaving school, I went to my grandma's house until it was time to leave. I stayed in my aunt Queen P's room and just talked on the phone and watched television. I planned to take advantage of my freedom when I wasn't doing that.

Then I heard a loud commotion. It was nighttime, and my grandmother was in her bedroom watching television. My Dad and his new girlfriend were sitting on a couch I had never seen before. My aunt Queen P and the big homie Ken-Den were on the other couch. As soon as I entered the living room, my father hit the woman he was with with a beer can upside her head. It sounded off "pow." Beer went everywhere, and then he jumped up and started punching her in the face, accusing her of staring at the Ken-Den too hard. I later discovered that this girlfriend was much younger than my father. She lived around the corner from us; her little sister was my homegirl from the turf, and her older brother was also an elder homie.

My aunt Queen P started screaming about calling the police. Ken Den and I laughed as we walked outside to enjoy a cigarette. By this time, it was late, and I figured my aunt, Queen

P, and big homie were leaving, so I asked them to drop me off at my mom's house.

It was always the same as usual back at my mom's house. My sisters would always be happy to see me (the earlier, the better) so we could watch movies. My mother was waiting to implement rules on me—chores or something else that would get on my nerves. She knew I was fresh out, so it must be a little later.

The next day in class, I sat back and peed at the white teacher, Sunshine. I would try and watch her without being caught by her or the students in the class.

The good thing about this school is that it is around the corner from the heart of my turf, and I could have someone come and get me every day. Today, it was the O.G. who liked to show off. He had a '66 Impala on hydraulics. I knew when he was in the parking lot because he wanted everybody in the strip mall to realize he was there. His music was blasting the Ghetto Boys, the bass making the room vibrate, followed by the sound of him making the car go up and down like he was at a car show. I loved that he was doing that because he was making my presence felt in a big way.

As soon as class was over, all eyes were on him. I walked over to him, and we gave each other the Skyline handshake, followed by showing love with a hug and a huge smile. This was his first time seeing me since I got out. I was putting it on thick, checking out his ride before hopping in. He hit the switch, and just like a gangster, he turned up the volume and swerved out of the lot.

Instead of going straight to my family's house, I decided to stop on the turf and see what the C.K. Riders had going on. Jason "Baby Skyline" Riley. He was still locked up, so I chilled at his house. I hadn't been spotted in the heart of the turf since I was out. I would ease through there because it was an immediate violation if I got caught hanging. I had missed the hood but dreaded returning to the system, trying like hell to get out.

However, I thought it was time to show my presence on the turf. Taking extreme risks for the homies—that's love.

After running inside the store and bumping into the homies, one minute turned into five. A few different homies came, and the next thing I knew, I was there for ten minutes. I felt the fame and glory and found myself hanging out much longer than I wanted.

Suddenly, the police hit the corner. I quickly walked into the store, where I knew I could hide for a minute. They kept it moving, and so did I. I got the hell out of the heart of the turf and walked over to my homegirl Muffin's house. Her mother was crazy, but because I was a regular around there, she talked that shit and let me in. Her mom loved me for sure.

She let me know all the goods that were going on in the heart of the set: who was in jail, who was out, who been hanging, and who can't ride, who's done jumped into the elite, and who done jumped off. A lot had changed since I was there last; she set me up with the latest and would send me on my way with releasing a fat nut. She was the one who took my virginity. She had some good sex and head. The trouble was it was community pussy, so I had to make sure I had the Jimmy on tight. Also, if you got caught over there too long, the homies would clown hard. We all were creeping, but if you got caught, it was a roast. That was a no-no. That shit would have your sex ratio going from one hundred to zero fast. So, like a thief in the night, I crept out of the house.

Later, when I was catching up with my mentor, a couple of the C.K. Riders were over there, getting ready to put in some work. Instantly, I could tell what was going on. I knew who was who, and immediately, my blood boiled. Like a dope fiend, I wanted some.

I was ready, and this was something I couldn't resist. My mentor handed me a strap and then asked if that one was good. "Hell yeah," I said, examining it. I pulled out the clip first, then evaluated everything on the weapon. I saw if the clip was fully loaded, looked for detail, and ensured it wasn't dirty or old. Cocked the chamber and looked through the barrel. It was ready to go, but I should've known that these dudes were serious about their business.

Feeling the firepower in my hands was like a dope fiend grabbing that needle for the first time in years. I felt the rush of my heartbeat, the eagerness to bust the gun; to feel it cock and bang, then spit out a shell, craving the loud sound of the bullets leaving the gun. Just like an Olympian in the last round, I was ready. Ready to gang bang and take the prize as the one who did the most.

The last guy pulled up, and the four of us went across the street and hopped into his two-door car. My mentors are Arnold' Young Bugs' Adkins and Billy 'CK Bill' Matthis. We jumped in the back seat. At first, it was quiet. Then CK Bill started rapping freestyle like he always did. I didn't give two shits about what he was doing because I was lost in my thoughts. Before I go on a mission, I think of every possible scenario except getting caught or the cops. But I think about the best way to do my thing and bust a move like an athlete prepares for a championship.

Our destination is Imperial Ave., Near the 4 Corners of Death. We hopped out on Imperial, and the homie driving said he was leaving. Imperial was on and popping at this time, and there was a lot of traffic.

First, we went to a location to meet after we put in work. Then we were to separate. Two homies went one way, and the other two went another. I was with Billy 'CK Bill' Matthis.

We hit the corner, and he said that one of our enemies was reported to hang over here around this time. If he showed up, we were going to knock him down. I was hoping that he was there. I had heard of him before and knew it would be a point up for our hood if we got him.

Then, we saw him standing outside his car with the driver's door open like he was about to hop in. He was talking to three people hanging around the steps, so we didn't think he would notice us heading over to him. But because we didn't have our hoodies on and our faces were out there, we didn't move.

Instead, the homie just said, "What's up, Blood? What is that woopty-woop like?" He threw up their gang sign, and they did the same. I could tell the one we were about to shoot at was trying hard to get a visual on us, I quickly put my head down. As soon as I picked my head up, it was a Blood from 5/9 Brims saying, what's up to the both of us? We both quickly said, what's up, blood? What is that South Like? I said. I told him my name was Brim Love. We introduced ourselves like we were from 5/9 Brims.

Just as soon as we left and returned around the corner, we discovered our hideout was compromised. We couldn't even get in. Thank God nothing happened.

Suddenly, the cops hit the corner and put the lights on us, and we all took off. The other three I was with were in tip-top shape because they ran, worked out regularly, and didn't do drugs or alcohol.

Before I knew it, we were all going in different directions. Luckily, I knew the area to a T because my family had stayed on all four corners. I ran through apartment after apartment, jumping fence after fence until I was at a location where I knew people I could hide out with. Nothing had happened, so I knew they weren't giving that kind of chase.

After standing up in holding for a few minutes, I noticed the homie returned to get us. This time, he was with his girl. She was a homegirl and a rat that messed with our rivals. I didn't like her and didn't want her to know my name or face.

After scooping us up, I got dropped off at my grandmother's house. I like that nothing happened that night because we weren't ready, and we would have been short if anything had gone down. I went to my aunt Queen and asked her to take me to my house. She agreed. I still had not caught up with my other aunt, Sis. It would be nice to see her, but I would have to wait until the weekend when I don't have to go to my mom's.

She was the aunt I would always live with, and I was hoping that if I got kicked out of my mother's house, I could stay with her again.

I entered my mother's house, and she acted nice and cool. I never knew who I would meet when dealing with her; sometimes, she would be cool, and sometimes she would have something up her butt. I was at ease when I bumped into the cool mom, but when that happened, I always figured she was about to con me into doing something else. That was why I kept my distance no matter what, but I was tired of dancing around the obvious. I knew the real her would emerge soon and wanted to prepare for it. If I weren't, I would have to bow down; that was the last thing I wanted to do. I didn't have anywhere else to go, and if she knew that, I could almost guarantee that she would be acting funny soon by pushing a hard line.

I had to contact my aunt Sis as soon as possible. I had to go to school the next day but planned to see her after leaving.

My Elementary School Kid didn't come to school often, which could have been because her dude knew that I was going there now. Either way, I was happy she didn't come to school because she could do extreme hating, contradicting my plan.

The white teacher, Sunshine, was starting to open up. I began to see her watching me out of the corner of her eye, even going as far as looking through the blinds at me. I would act as if I didn't see her. At first, I didn't know what it was and wouldn't make a move until I did because a lot rested on me getting with her. She could have been intrigued, curious, and sceptical of my presence. Was it because she wanted to give me a go and taste the thrill of being with a gangster, or was she afraid of me? I knew I was putting it on real thick, but I hoped I wasn't doing too much to run Sunshine off.

By now, she most definitely knew that I was a real-deal gangster. Some days, I would plan for my homies to come and get me, but other times, the homies come and get me without asking. But the way it all coincided made me feel and look like I was a young Veteran. Every day, I had a different homie or O.G. coming to pick me up, and they would always open the door to see what it looked like in the classroom. By doing this, they would make the entire class nervous. I ate it all up because it was what I had been banging for love, respect, and honour. I was being spoiled to the fullest by some young gangsta.

That's the funny thing about it with me, and that's why I wouldn't allow them to talk about my loved ones when I was down. I didn't call or ask for much then. I looked at it from a different angle, which made much sense. I didn't call on them to look out for me with letters, pictures, and what have you. That wasn't a guy thing, and I knew if I was out there, that wasn't some stuff that I was going to be doing for a homie, either. If I were on the streets, I would be gang-banging and chasing money and sex. Who would have the time to write letters, take pictures, and all that stuff when he was an active gangster? Once I was back on the soil of my turf, I wanted my love and attributes. That is exactly how I felt during my hard times, and staying solid for representing the Piru gang. This is why I banged with such vigour and why they showed up without me asking.

It wasn't the homies I ran with growing up but the older ones I desired to hang with since I was young on the set. It wasn't an easy crew to be a part of; you had to put in real work and recruit honest workers to provide Rider services. I'd heard stories of the homie Billy 'CK Bill' Matthis being a Rider and active, and now I was hanging and bangin' with him regularly. I admired Arnold 'Young Bugs' Adkins for his finesse, style, and grace. The girls used to be all over him; I wore his jersey for football practice, and all the girls surrounded me like a pop star. The homies loved him, and enemies feared him. I still remember when the C.K. Riders were getting ready to go across town and fight with the enemies. They weren't willing to take anyone that might lose, so if you couldn't get with them, you couldn't go. Then the fade began. I understood fully what he meant and what he was doing and learned when to take my shot at pushing lines.

The last time I was out, I met up with some homies. We were on our way to put in some work for the set, but all the crews went their separate ways on missions. At that time, my team and I were being watched by my elders. To see who we were and what we were all about. We were too young to be fully trusted by the elders. They needed to see who we were as the next generation of C.K. Riders. I wanted us to be more feared, respected, famous, and active than the elder crew. I knew I had stepped up my game to be banging with the next generation, but it would have to go up another level.

The last time I was out, I was still doing drive-byes. Now, it would be up close and personal. I was hungry for that dose and had many dreams about it while doing time. I needed to be on my A-game to do this type of riding because a lot of running, jumping, pushing, and pulling would be involved. To have the pleasure and honour to be in this crew was an achievement in the highest regard in my mind.

Chapter 5

'On My Mama'

I went to Uncle A's house to hang with Trigger Happy and his associates. Uncle A worked mornings, so his house would be off the hook during those times. I didn't like some of the dudes my relative hung with simply because they hadn't been put to the test—you had to be in the same type of activities to be in my presence. But it was easy to hang when you had all the essentials to help you act like a gangster. There were plenty of guns, so they didn't have to break into houses, and they didn't have to steal cars because my relative would. That's why when I hung over there, I would be distant.

Trigger Happy had some girls that stayed in National City. One of the girls had a friend that was with the fake Crip that Lazy Larry Trigger Happy hung with. I saw her that night; she was stunningly pretty in the face and thick like a king-size Snickers. I had to have her.

Trigger Happy said, "That's my homie's girl."

I laughed. "Fool, forget your homie. I got to have me some of that."

I got to her and asked her for her number. She declined. We were moving around at a fast pace. She was not trying to give it up. But after some persistence, she gave in. I promised to call her later.

We left as fast as we came.

Back at Uncle A's house, we were hanging out. My homeboy Fidgety picked us up in a car he had just got. It was a bucket, but it was his car, and it was exactly what we needed then. We went to the Pinkies and hung out there for a while. Krafty's dude went to jail, and now Trigger Happy was sexing her. This dude was acting like he was spying on the girl.

It was late, and Krafty said we had to leave her apartment, but she didn't mean everybody. After she said that, she started singling people out. I was one of those people. I was hot about it, but I was madder about Trigger Happy. He wanted some sex; forget everything else. His response should have been, "If he leaves, I leave." He thought he would shut the door, return inside the house, and chill.

Me and Fidgety left and came back in five minutes. I knocked on the door. First, they refused to open it. I kept banging on the door until I heard someone yelling behind it.

"You're going to get us kicked out if you keep banging on the door!"

I said, "Get Trigger Happy. Make him answer the door."

Finally, he opened it, and I ran in after him. I tackled him over the couch, wrapping my arms around him before me, and Fidgety dragged him down three flights of stairs and into the back of the car. I held him down in the back seat until we got to my grandmother's house, which was just around the corner and down the road.

We hopped out and squared off in the middle of the street. Because we were family, he knew what defenses to use on me—but I knew the same about him. He danced around in the street and wouldn't square up. Without ever connecting a punch, and my grandmother, Pops, and aunties outside. The family stopped it. I screamed at him and them: "If one goes, we all go!"

After all the madness, me and Fidgety hopped into his car and left, and he dropped me off at my mother's house.

Once I arrived, I attempted to stay out of her way and hope she stayed out of mine. She always had something to complain about under her breath, especially the chores she wanted me to do around the house, even though I never dirtied up anything and would barely shower there. I got it. She wished I would leave because she didn't want me using her home as a spot, and that's all it was for me. It was a place to be safe, without worry and stress—a place for peace while sleeping, a must to escape the trials and tribulations of the fast lane. If I were confined to it twenty-four hours a day, it would drive me crazy. If you can't sleep without being able to relax, what kind of sleep is that? I knew being at my mother's provided me with at least that.

But I felt I was grown, and soon enough, I would be leaving my place. First was school, a job, and being a Rider. I planned to get some crack, crystal, and PCP to sell. Because my family smoked crack, they had a lot of friends who smoked, too. I like to be as low as possible while selling dope. But I had to stabilize my living situation, so I would stay at my grandma's house to sell the bulk. Another one of my favourite locations was in the Tops: Meadowbrook Apartments, Skyline Park, and Gribble St.

Times have changed, and the first thing to do is play peep games. I stole cars and broke into houses like the last time I was on the streets. Now, it felt beneath me unless I was guaranteed to come up on a sweet lick. I had many plans, and the small stuff didn't matter.

After about a month, my mother and I came to that place where it was time to move on. I would miss her and my sisters, but we were better apart. My dad arrived, and I couldn't wait to leave.

I can't put the abuse I'd taken from her mentally, physically, and emotionally into words.

I was about to get on a different road. Where this highway would take me, I didn't know.

I went to my grandma's house first to unwind and gather my thoughts for my next move. Pop said I could parole there if I needed to; it was the perfect place because all my relatives were not there. Either way, I wasn't quite ready to live there yet—not with a paper trail. I would stick to the program and go to Aunt Sis' house. There were a couple of things that I didn't like about staying with Aunt Sis, but it was still safer than Grandma's or my mother's house.

Aunt Sis stayed in Spring Valley on Grand St. The street was constantly popping, but not with the mischief I had in mind. Apartments lined both sides, and the interior was ghetto—exactly where I wanted to be. Across the street was a 7/11 with many young girls hanging around, which was a plus. The bus stops were far from where she lived; it was a significant inconvenience, but other than that, it was doable. My aunt was an alcoholic and a functioning smoker. Because she dabbled in crack, she had many associates. She wouldn't be sweating me for anything that I was doing. It would take a few days to iron out all the tension of having a new roommate, but we would be all good once the bugs were worked out.

At school, the teacher Sunshine and I have been sneaking and peeking at each other. After school, she would give students regular rides. Today, she looked good, and I knew I would have to go all the way. I was tired of playing.

I was the first one to the car. When the other students tried to hop in, I said, "Not today, family. We're going in a different direction." They were all mad, as expected. I didn't care about that. I would run some tests on her to see how wide open the door is for me to go through.

First, I removed her music from the radio and put it in my music: *1990-Sick* by Spice 1. Then I cranked the volume to the max, only turning it down to give her directions to where I was going. We drove through my community, and as we stopped on Skyline and Meadowbrook at the lights, I turned down the radio and said, "You're thick, juicy, and look damn good."

She looked at me like *I'm your teacher*, but she said nothing. I took this as a sign to take it a step further. As we drove down Skyline Drive, I reached over and put my hand on her thigh. Silently, she let me keep it there, so I massaged it, grabbing and rubbing it up and down. She was hot and ready when we pulled into my grandma's driveway. She slammed the transmission into the park, and I leaned over and stuck my tongue in her mouth. After a minute of kissing, we stopped. She quickly pulled out a pen and paper and put her number on it. I took my Rider music from her radio and jumped out of the car like a gangster.

Walking to the front door, I turned around and watched her leave, telling myself I would call her tonight. I stepped into the house feeling elated. The plan was coming together. Thinking about it made me hard as a rock; I couldn't wait until later. I would call her when it was lovely and dark.

In the meantime, I went to Uncle A's house in Encanto. I came at the right time because they were talking about getting a double-up in crack. Uncle A's girl gave me a hundred dollars for it. I told her after I flipped it a few times, I would give her back her money. She wanted the cash back sooner rather than later, but I told her that she knew the deal and would have to wait.

A day later, I went over there, and my uncle talked about giving back the money his baby mama loaned me. As promised, I told him I would, but they should let me flip it again. He was talking all kinds of crap. I knew I couldn't tell him the real reason she was tripping. He stared at me crazy.

I said in a stern voice, "Look, you will get the money back when I'm done flipping. I'm not going to rob you, Uncle. She and I had a deal, and you don't know the specifics."

I walked into the house and saw my relative's girlfriend sitting on the couch with her relative, the one who was with Lazy Larry. Turns out he was outside. She was sitting on my lap when he came back into the house. I dared him to say anything to me. He didn't. He returned to the house to pout like a girl, throwing his beer on the ground.

Uncle A came inside the house to check on the situation. He looked at me and asked, "Why did you do that to the boy?" I paid him no attention, and neither did the girl. A few minutes later, she and her relative left. My uncle continued cracking jokes long after they were gone. My uncle was more upset about his beer being wasted than anything. We all laughed.

It was lovely and dark now, and I had other things on my mind. I called my grandmother to come and get me from my uncle's house. As soon as they arrived, my grandmother started making a fuss about me paying my uncle the money. I guess he told everybody about it. But I was still angry about how my grandmother robbed me of my money. I'd been laying low, waiting to check the hell out of her.

Like a gangster, I walked up to her side of the car directly in front of me. I leaned down, got eye-to-eye with her, and whispered, "You stay out of any business of mine. You don't involve yourself, not unless I involve you. If you ever get in my business again, there will be some problems." I stared at her like she was a Crip. She just stared at me blankly and didn't say a word.

I jumped in the back seat. I wanted to ensure that she and anyone around my company knew I wasn't the same person who went in—I was ten times worse. I wasn't playing any games with anybody. I'd get respect by any means and take it if they didn't give it to me. She and my aunt understood.

After returning to her house, I called Sunshine and asked her to get me to hang out. She said yes, and she was on her way. I was elated that the must-needed piece to my puzzle was coming together. I never had sex at the beach, so I didn't know who to go to. I hoped she did because I was ready to beat that sweet nectar. I could see the imprint of her twat through her pants, and it was chunky.

She came twenty minutes later. I stuck my tongue in her mouth as soon as I got into her car. I put my music on the stereo, sat back to recline, and drove away.

I said, "Let's go to the beach." The entire way there, I was massaging her thigh with my hand. Then after a while, I just turned in my seat and began rubbing her pussy through her jeans. By the time we got to our destination, I was hot and bothered, ready to jump her bones on the spot. I had to get a grip on myself.

We got out, walked to the beach, and looked at the water. We talked for a few. Something about the water made me relax and drift into thought. After talking, I was ready for what we had come for. It was time to have sex.

She got on the passenger side, and I got in after her. We did the kissing and pulling her clothes off at the same time deal. She had a nice body, but tonight was not the time for loving. I stuck my boner deep inside her tight box, as deep as it would allow me to go. I got a couple more inches by putting her legs on my shoulders. I was banging hard, digging deep into her love nest. I looked deep into her eyes, attempting to sex her soul. Through her eyes, I could tell that she was loving it. The windows fogged up, and the whole car rocked back and forth. I didn't care if anyone could see us. After twenty minutes of some severe sexing, we were dripping in sweat. It was time to release this nut.

When we were done, I got out of the car and looked around. There was a dude close by who looked like he saw our car rocking and rolling. I was full of myself. Cocky as hell, I jumped in the driver's seat and started the car. She had a stick shift hatchback, and I wanted to show her I could drive. She said nothing, sitting back and allowing me to handle my business.

I drove to Aunt Sis' house in Spring Valley. When we arrived, my aunt asked Sunshine to get a beer even though she had never met her. The teacher did it with no problem. Before she left, I told her I would be in touch, then gave her a kiss and a slap on the butt, and she was gone.

Aunt Sis said, "She is a keeper."

"Of course she is," I said. "Until I graduate."

The trouble with having a crack sack when you stay with dope fiends is they always want some, and most of the time, on credit, and they try and make it hard to say no since you're not paying any bills. This is how my Aunt Sis got at me and made me feel some way. She would pay me back most of the money but then complain about the bills so that I would pay them. Living with crackheads was always an adventure, but Aunt Sis wasn't that bad; I have lived with worse.

Living with her, I saw some of the funniest things crackheads do. One crackhead would be all up her butt, following her from room to room, begging to hump her feet. I don't know what he saw in her feet, but to me, she had some of the ugliest feet I ever saw. She had another crackhead that would take a hit, get naked, and dive into the closet. Both these dudes were friends of the family I've known my entire life. I would sit back and watch all this crap like it was in a movie. It was surreal. This was the life for me; never a dull moment. However, I did miss being able to have some peace while sleeping.

At school, the mood between Sunshine and I had changed. She was always watching me now. I didn't want anything to change between us in class, so I planned to ignore her as much as possible. If the rest of the students found out what we had going on, it wouldn't be good for her, me, or my plan.

During this time, I would do half the work in whatever book I was in. Then, I would copy the rest from Hershey. I would turn in my work and get it back with five credits and an A+. The girl I was cheating off of would turn in the same book and get 2.5 credits and a B+.

Hershey started saying, "I think she is digging on you."

I would say, "No, not me."

I knew then that if I copied Hershey, I wouldn't let her see my grade and credits received. I didn't stop cheating on her; after all, I was trying to graduate as soon as possible.

Sunshine was friendly and kind-hearted with a banging body. Elementary School Kids would barely come to school. Now and then, an Elementary School Kid would do some sexing. She would give me her pager, but then having it would come with drama from her dude. I didn't stay near her anymore. Plus, she was on the shot and wasn't getting pregnant anytime soon. She no longer had a role in my plans, plots, and schemes. Slowly but surely, she and I fizzled out.

Chapter 6

Block Monster

Back at my uncle's A's house, I'd returned the money I borrowed, so we were again on good terms. Now that they knew my word was my bond, our relationship improved. I needed that bond with Uncle A; he had the firepower I would need. Plus, I had to be able to come and go from there like it was another one of my houses. I didn't have a key to the place, but I acted as if I did.

While hanging out one day, the homeboy pulled up in a U-Haul truck with his buddy, talking about riding on some cross towns. I didn't know this dude, but heard of him while down. But nothing worthy of me riding with him, so I wasn't into that. I was sceptical. Besides that, it was a must that I run a check on his resume since I was fresh out from doing years.

I called my mentor, and he said, "Hell to the no. The dude is alright, but when you go on a mission, he thinks every car is the cops. From experience, I know that throws a monkey wrench in the program."

I went back outside and told them nothing was happening. I looked him in the eye and said, "Blood, I don't know you." Then he and the dude he came with left.

Now that I was selling crack, I needed to get a spot to post up at in the Pinkies. One night, hanging in the apartments, the homie took me to a place where he posted up and always left with a plate to go. He took me here several times, but tonight, they had some relatives from Detroit visiting.

One had caught my eye. She was older than me, with two kids already, a girl and a newborn boy. The trouble with messing with an older female is that they're full of crap and play games. We all mobbed to Encanto park. It was there she and I got acquainted. That night, she did my hair, and we ended up sexing. After that, I posted more in the Pinkies now that I had somewhere to stash my crack.

One night, I was lounging in the cut watching—something I always did—when I saw some unknown faces coming through. Their movement was gangster-like. I began to see who was intruding on our territory on the low. I looked around for any witnesses. I pulled my gun, put a bullet in the chamber, and reached to pull my mask down. Just as I did, they started moving quickly to get out of there. Trigger Happy was on the way. As soon as they hopped in their car, Trigger Happy hit the corner in Fidgety's car. Trigger Happy began blasting, chasing them out of the area and screaming at the top of his lungs, dissing hoods. This was the first time something like that happened while I was around, but not the last.

When that happened, I stopped liking Krafty. She didn't know what she was doing and would eventually get somebody killed or hurt. She didn't understand the nature of the game to the fullest. Every time I went into her apartment, I was on watch. Still, Trigger Happy was sparked on her. Me and Detroit were still hitting it off cool. I was over at the apartment she shared with her family a lot. I was hustling crack, attempting to move up in quantity.

Later that night, while sleeping, I awoke to Detroit moving up and down on me. First, I thought I was being robbed for the dope I had in my ass cheeks. Finally opening my eyes fully, Detroit was on me, riding me like a bull. I wasn't even hard or inside her.

She said, "Go back to sleep, go back to sleep."

I said, "Hold up, baby, let me get hard and put it in."

With a bit of resistance, she allowed me to, but she was slightly agitated like I was messing up what she had going on. I couldn't even stay awake. After two minutes, I fell back to sleep inside her vagina. My penis went soft; she was happy and kept going.

Eventually, she woke me up because of how hard she was exploding on my penis. I opened my eyes a little bit and thought I was tripping.

The following day, I woke up thinking that it was a dream. Detroit was smiling and laughing like she had the time of her life. I asked her, "What was that?"

She said she was rubbing her clit against the shaft of my dick. That is what gave her a nut like that. I thought, damn, that was different. She was older than me by a few years, so I chalked it up to experience.

Chapter 7

'Hear From Me'

After leaving school. I was at the bus stop next to the Meadowbrook apartments in the heart of my territory. Before I got on the bus, the police hit the corner and saw me. They allowed the bus to leave but followed behind. When we beat Skyline and Meadowbrook, two cops walked onto the bus and asked me to leave. I looked at them, confused.

I asked, "Did I do something, officer?"

After a few seconds, the taller one said, "Sir, can you please get off the bus?"

I knew they wouldn't let me go, and I didn't want to hold everyone up, so I slowly walked off the bus like I was walking the plank.

Once off the bus, the shorter cop asked, "Is your name Onaje Barbee?" I couldn't believe it. Immediately, I knew that this was going to end badly.

I instinctively said, "No, sir."

The one questioning me had been on the force for a while. He was the one in charge here. He asked again, "Are you Onaje Barbee?"

I said, "No, sir."

He rolled up my sleeves and said, "Let me see. He should have a CK tattoo on his arm." There wasn't one. That juvenile hall scratch tattoo was long gone.

The taller cop said, "There isn't no CK tattoo," as both shone their flashlights all over me.

Then, the smaller one jumped on the computer in their squad car and called out, "He should have a Piru tattoo on his other arm." They began looking for that tattoo. Again, they couldn't find it.

"I told you that isn't me," I said. "What have I done, officer?" But they weren't hearing anything I had to say. They would book me and put me in jail by any means.

Then the officer jumped back into the car and said, "He might have a slash across his stomach. Bottom left." They lifted my shirt, and there it was: a significant slash crossing the left side of my stomach—that smile every bad guy hated to see crossed the cop's face.

He looked at me and said, "Hello there, Mr. Onaje Barbee. Why have you got us going through all this crap?"

I asked, "Why are you messing with me? I'm coming from school."

The smaller cop said, "You shouldn't be going through Skyline."

"I'm going to my grandmother's house."

"We're going to let you talk to your parole officer about that," he said, placing me in the squad car's back seat.

It was the longest ride ever. I thought to myself, *Here we go again. I'm on my way back to CYA.* And there was no telling when I would get back out because I'd have to go through a panel again.

We stayed at the police station for a while. Then, we made the long trip to the juvenile hall. I knew I messed up, but at the same time, I didn't understand how they could take me in for riding a bus through Skyline—a stupid violation. I didn't think it to be this serious.

I fell asleep on the bench I was handcuffed to. After more than a few hours, they woke me up. The next process was the long ride I always liked. Because you're about to be taken from society, it is your last glimpse of the outside world.

We got to the juvenile hall late. The staff recognized my name on the door and immediately stopped by to say hello. It had been a few years since I'd last seen them. They got me in and out of receive and release in an hour or so. That usually takes a lot longer. Like a professional criminal, I was too comfortable and relaxed during the entire process.

I was back in the maximum-security unit 1400. I asked, "Why am I in this unit?"

"Because you've been to CYA, you'll never return to the regular unit," they answered. My level of expertise was above and beyond the halls. That sucked because it would mean a hard time.

They opened the door to the cell block. I walked in, sat down against the wall, and waited for the staff to assign me to a one-person cell. After five minutes, they walked me to my cell. I heard the familiar sound of the door opening. It made all that I was going through too real.

I was mad at the system, furious at the cops, angry at myself, and mad at the parole officer for not letting me out. I overheard my parole officer talking to the cops earlier. He told them to take me to the hall, and he would get it figured out. They let me know that I was nothing but a number and they could do anything they wanted.

I would have to be a lot sharper and brighter regarding my freedom if they let me out. I knew that they were being too strict when it came to me being in Skyline. My entire family stayed in the Skyline area. That obstacle made no sense at all, and it put me in positions I couldn't get away from—a way to keep us locked up. I was totally convinced of that.

I relaxed and started getting my head in the game. I was mad at myself for not doing any work for the set while out. Most days, I was deep in thought, trying to figure out how to escape this mess. I lied to the police officer when I gave him a false name. Why was I being treated special? However, I wanted to make some things work with the tools I had. Instead of concentrating on the negative, I began thinking of the positives at my disposal.

I had my teacher, Sunshine. I called my family to get in touch with her and let her know to contact my parole officer. I wanted her to speak on my behalf for the school program. A couple of days later, I began to get letters from her. She insisted she was being persistent in the pursuit of my release.

Because I had not been out that long, it all was natural for me—my habitat. Within a couple of days, I was jailing like normal. I was in maximum security and stuck in the cell for twenty-three hours daily. After my release, I consumed my time with books, magazines, working out, and thoughts of tearing the streets up. I knew one thing for sure: I was staying out of Skyline. It's not passing through. Not hanging. If somebody caught up with me, it wouldn't be there.

Two weeks later, in the afternoon, my cell door popped open. I poked my head out the door and heard, "Barbee, pack up your stuff. You're released." I couldn't believe it. I had not spoken with anyone, so whatever the teacher told them worked.

Smiling from ear to ear, I grabbed my things and exited ASAP. I walked to the receive and release and changed into my street clothes. They gave me bus fare, and I got away from there as fast as possible.

My little relative Gino 'Lunatick' Langston was simultaneously getting out of the group home. He needed to parole to his mother's house, where I was staying. Now I had to move to my grandmother's house in the heart of Skyline, which was perfect for me. What could my parole officer say about that now? It was time to get active, and staying far away wouldn't work. I needed more sex, guns, money, and access. It was clear the cops were on to me, and they wanted me off the streets. I would have to play this game differently if I wanted to stay out long enough to tear the streets up.

That night, I got a call from Toons. He asked me to stop by and check him out. When we got to his house, I met his homie, Dimes, and we heard some music bumping loud from across the street.

"Who stays over there?" I asked Toons.

He said, "I saw some girls over there a few times."

"We're going over there to see what's up."

Toons had another homie with him named Dimes.

I knocked on the front door. They didn't answer, and the music was blasting. I banged on the door like the cops. *Bang, bang, bang!* The door swung open, but not wide enough for us to see inside the house.

A tall Black dude mean-mugging us said, "What's up, Blood?" with aggression in his voice. Immediately, I felt the hatred. I knew they weren't from our side of town.

"What's up, Piru?" I said with matching hostility. "What's popping in there?" A couple of dudes came to the door, and the music went down.

The guy at the door said, "You can come in for five dollars a head."

Then another dude added, "And a pat down for guns," while giving us a crazy look.

Immediately, we all took offence. "On Piru, we are not paying no money, and we are not getting patted down," I said. "We're allowing you to have a party on our turf, on Piru."

Now, they started to feel our tension and switched it up. By this time, we all were too far gone. I couldn't believe the audacity of these fools talking blasphemy on our turf.

Then Toons said, "We're not broke gangstas. We got $20 for you." Me and Dimes were highly upset. I began to tell them

88

dudes that they were acting like Crips. More of them came to the door, looking to see if we had reinforcements around the corner. They wouldn't come from inside the house. I don't know what they were thinking, but we were strapped and wanted warfare.

The homie Dimes said, "Bow down to Skyline, fool! Bow down! Bow down to Skyline!" repeatedly. The tenth time he said it, someone pushed past the doorman and hit Dimes with a right cross. Dimes was trying to pull his gun out of his pocket. During their scuffle, Dimes' pistol fell to the ground, unbeknownst to us. I hit the dude fighting Dimes with a forty bottle over the head, and he fell on top of Dimes just as someone unloaded rounds into his back. We rolled the dude off Dimes and picked him up.

We started running to Fidgety's car, parked in front of the house. Just as we made our way there, another dude ran out of the house, grabbed Dimes' gun, and started shooting at us. Now, behind the car, we hit back. He was ducking and running around for cover, and after a full minute of shooting at each other, we got out of there.

We ran away from the scene as fast as possible, hoping to make it to Dimes' house since he lived the closest. As soon as we got there, we ducked into his garage and heard the sound of the helicopter making its way toward the action. We laid low for a long minute.

An hour later, Fidgety, Gino 'Lunatick' Langston, and I felt we could make it to my grandmother's house since she didn't stay far from where we were. Because the police station was just up the hill and they were coming and going from the crime scene, we quickly snuck through our neighbour's backyards to get there. Finally, we made it and snuck into the bedroom window in the backyard. We laughed and high-fived each other, overjoyed by the night's festivities.

Later that evening, Fidgety wanted to go home. Gino 'Lunatick' Langston and I kept telling him not to go, but he insisted. I kept saying, "Piru, if you do that, the police will take you to jail ASAP." I told him they would be waiting for him when he got there because the car parked at the incident was registered to him. He didn't think so and was adamant about going home. Eventually, he got a ride and left.

In the wee hours of the morning, we tried to call him, and he didn't answer. I knew then that it was all bad. I told Gino, "The police got your boy." He didn't believe me, but I was right.

Later that day, Fidgety flew to my house at high speed. He jumped out of his car with his finger to his lips and said, "Don't say a word because they're listening." Fidgety, Shorty, and I walked up to the power plant from my grandmother's house to talk because he insisted his car was bugged.

I said, "What's up?"

"They know that we didn't do anything," he answered.

"What?" I asked. "Who's 'they'? Calm down and tell me everything that happened from the beginning."

"They asked me if you were there," he said.

"Who?"

"The police put a picture of you in front of me and asked if Onaje Barbee was there," he explained. I stared at him. "I said yes, but that you didn't do anything. They asked if Gino was there too, and I said he didn't do anything either."

"Why did they put our picture in front of you?" I asked.

He said, "I don't know. They didn't put any pictures but you two in front of me."

"How is it that we didn't do anything if someone got shot!" I said. Still, he insisted that it went the way he said it.

The sun was setting now, so he went to take a piss. I pulled out my burner and approached him as soon as he did. Shorty dropped to his knees and said, "Don't smoke the homie! Don't kill the homie!" I figured if I shot him, I would have to shoot Shorty, and that's why he brought him along. Coming to my senses, I looked around, tucked my pistol in my pants, and then returned to my grandmother's house. I knew it wouldn't be long before some form of the law was on its way.

They came the next morning looking for guns and any other type of paraphernalia that could put me back in jail. They didn't find anything. I had to report to my parole officer as soon as possible, and he put me on house arrest, stating that he wanted to see where this case was going.

I had a girlfriend named Chocolate who lived around the corner from my grandmother's house. She picked me up so I could go around and let the others involved know the situation. Fidgety said he said nothing about them because they didn't know about them. Why were they asking questions about us? How did they know about us? Gino 'Lunatick' Langston and I were fresh out. I knew they were going to come and holler at him. They did, and he got locked up and then released in a couple of weeks.

I was now being home-schooled. Since I was no longer going to continue, I figured there was no more need for the teacher and stopped talking to Sunshine.

I went on house arrest and got a job at the shipyard, allowing me to come and go with minimum freedom. But I didn't care; I was happy I could get away from the house during the day since they would give me some time to get home from the job. Sometimes, I would get there early with enough time to do other stuff, like go around the corner and get some sex from Chocolate.

Chocolate was in the same grade as me in Morse High School. She was good with schoolwork and would do mine for me. I met her at a house party while hanging with the homies from G.P.M. (Getting Pussy & Money). She was thick as a snicker, short, with long hair. I thought she would be a good candidate for having my baby. Her family was one of the well-off families in our area. Back then, I didn't believe that I would escape a life in jail or a death sentence. So, I would attempt to choose a female that I felt would be capable without me. After checking enough of my boxes off, I begin trying to have a kid with her. She stayed with her grandparents, and they went to sleep early, so I would sneak into the first floor of their two-story house after they went to bed.

The shipyard that I worked at was Southwest Marine, near downtown. I worked as a fire watch at the foot of Sampson St. but didn't stay there long before transferring to North Island on Coronado Island. Gangsters would wear their colour bandanna to represent their side of town under their hard hats. I did the same. I talked to nobody but who I had to. I liked nobody.

I worked on the USS *Kitty Hawk* and the USS *Constellation*. I liked The *Kitty Hawk* more because it was co-ed, and I thought

MR. ONAJE M. BARBEE SR.

I had more action at becoming a military woman. My hair started getting long, and I thought I was the flyest guy. They must've seen me watching ladies because they moved me to the *Constellation*.

My mother would call me like an alarm clock every morning at 4 a.m. She'd be over by 4:30 and would have me to work before 5 a.m. I had two supervisors that were directly above me, who I saw every day before work. One was an electrician who was an affiliate of my Skyline community. He was Filipino and grew up with a homie named Timmy, with whom I played football with. He ended up helping me out in a significant way. He would tell me to get lost on the boat and to check in periodically.

Then there was the welder on crystal meth. He would first find his assigned spot. Then he would stop and pull out a line of meth and snort it. He would look at me with glossy eyes and say, "I'm good. You can find a bunker to watch videos, nap, or whatever. Check back in with me later. Just leave your fire extinguisher." I would leave my fire extinguisher, find an empty bunker, and watch rap videos until I passed out. Then, I would get up and walk around.

I would trip off how huge those ships were. I never thought they were that big on the inside, with walkways going up and down and all the way through. They had a kitchen off the hook with a buffet serving fresh fruit, meat, salads, seafood, and everything else. I would slide through there and grab all kinds of stuff. The store was nice and cheap with no taxes. I started shopping and cashing my checks there. I would be in the smoking alley, messing around with all the Navy men, cracking jokes. The dudes smoke cigarettes every five minutes. I would travel through the entire ship, making easy money every day.

The trouble with that job is that once you get near your 90-day mark, they would fire you and then hire you again for the same stuff. That way, you didn't get any benefits. It was all a game, just like the rest of the world, unless you had a trained skill. It didn't matter much to me as long as I made money. I was still selling crack and stacking up a nice penny while on house arrest.

Chapter 8

'That Pressure'

Me and Billy "CK Bill" Matthis began hanging tough when I got off house arrest. He had guns like I had guns, so it was only fitting we came together like butt cheeks. He would pull up in the best-stolen cars for us to stalk the streets in, and being with him taught me a lot about our craft of a Rider's rampage.

This guy was in great shape. He would go jogging regularly and drink orange juice every day, and he didn't drink alcohol or do drugs. Other than that, he loved fighting and shooting; he loved it even more when the odds were against him. CK Bill was the epitome of fearless.

One night, we had trouble finding these dudes in a rival neighbourhood. We'd be patrolling in a vehicle or walking through their perimeters but weren't having any luck catching them—especially the ones we wanted. So we met with the rest of the crew and decided to go through in the morning.

I wasn't even thinking about riding because we were in a car that I bought. We had one gun in case it didn't go well, but not to ride. I was driving, Gino "Lunatick" Langston was in the backseat, and CK Bill was in the passenger seat. We hit the corner in our rival hood where 15-20 dudes were hanging out, completely oblivious to anything except themselves. Completely relaxed.

I knew it would get good when we came back tomorrow with reinforcements.

The scene gave CK Bill a hard-on immediately. He couldn't control himself and started jumping around in his seat. The closer we got, the more it seemed like he was busting a nut. He started talking to himself, almost in a whisper, as he saw people he'd been looking for since his release from CYA. His upper body was out the window when we got near the dude hanging out. Of course, they noticed him hanging there, and when they recognized him, they started flipping him off and trying to spit on him.

CK Bill pulled out the gun and started blasting in their direction. We kept going around the bend until we reached a four-way stop sign. When we pulled up, there was a cop car on our left. CK Bill whispered, "Punch it, punch it."

"Kick back, Piru," I replied as I put on the right blinker, hoping the police would leave first so I could go in a different direction.

They didn't budge.

I couldn't wait. I turned right slowly, watching the cops through the rear-view mirror while trying hard not to turn my head and make it obvious. The cop drove into the middle of the four-way and stopped, debating what to do. I could tell they didn't know if they should follow us or go toward the crowd where they heard the shooting come from.

After a minute, they went towards the shots. I made the first left, and just as I did, over a small lump of a hill, I could see a cop car's lights. I made a U-turn and pulled in front of a house.

I said, "Duck!" They did. I acted as if I were waiting for someone to come outside, careful not to look in the cop's direction when they passed.

As soon as they were out of sight, I drove off, telling them to stay down till we were well away from the area, hitting every back street to the nearest freeway.

I realized then that the homie CK Bill was a spur-of-the-moment type, a loose cannon. I would have to watch myself when gang-banging with him, but it wouldn't be easy because he was my big homie. I was so star-struck that I wouldn't allow anything to stop me from banging with him.

We returned to the turf to review what happened with a few other members of the CK Riders. My mentor didn't want me to ride with CK Bill anymore because he was like a crash dummy; one day, he would crash and wreck both of us.

"The homie only sees one way when it comes to riding," he said. "Go 100%."

We had blown the spot and messed everything up. If CK Bill *did* hit anything, it wasn't a K, so it was a busted mission. Knowing my mentor, he was mad at himself, which wasn't good for anybody. All I knew was that I wanted to make it right ASAP.

After putting my life on the line for a life sentence, the first thing I would do was contact a girl for some intense sexual healing—the freakier, the better. So I called Hoe Bear. She was a big girl—always had been—and pretty in the face, born and raised on the block where our set hung. The mole on her cheek made her angelic features stand out. Although she was younger than me, she was more mature sexually. Plus, her tight twat was some of the best I'd ever had. Her baby daddy was locked up, so she would allow me to hang at her spot when things got hot for me.

Every time she and I would have sex, it was like the second time. We were never boyfriend and girlfriend, but no matter who she was with, she always found the time to give me a dose of that tight, wet goodness.

That night, she had some excellent smoke to take on. I drank my usual Thunderbird and cherry Kool-Aid. Bone Thugs-n-Harmony's "Choosey Lover" blasted on repeat all night. She knew what I was on and what I had been up to just by soaking up my energy. She insisted I did nothing but sip on my drink while she pleasured me.

Holding my bottle, I sat on a chair with my clothes off. She was teasing my penis by gently kissing the head, then flicking her tongue in and out of the hole at the tip while looking at me with the seduction of an experienced queen. Then she gently stroked me, still holding my gaze. She kissed it, then sucked, then kissed, then sucked while cupping my ball sack. I put the bottle to my lips, taking my last sip. She was making me go crazy with excitement that I never felt before. I put the top on the bottle, and she still had total control, refusing to let go. I dropped the bottle on the floor. She pulled my penis out of her mouth with a *pop*.

I went to the bed and lay flat on my back while she opened my legs and put my balls into her mouth, stroking my penis. It took everything in me not to explode. Feeling the intensity in my legs, she stopped and kissed my thighs, stomach, and chest. She learned a lot while I was away.

She climbed on top and stayed there for hours, knowing just when to pull out before I exploded, then switching it around by making me feel her super tight cat with a different stroke. It felt so good that I eventually begged her to let me bust. Finally, after hours, she did, taking it all inside her. We did this all night into the wee hours of the morning. It was exactly what I needed to get on with the get-down of being a Rider.

Later that afternoon, Trigger Happy said, "Big bro, I got some broads on the way—some Crip girls from West Coast. There's five of them so that we can take our pick." He slid closer and said, "You know that Crip you fought in Campo?"

"Which Crip from West Coast?" I asked. "I fought more than one."

"Look at her," he said. "She looks just like him."

I checked her out, and the resemblance was unmistakable. She was a sexy piece named Lovely with a caramel complexion like she could be a mixture of Black and something else. She had long, curly hair with dimples on her cheeks, juicy titties, thick thighs, and a tight little butt. Immediately, she and I locked eyes.

My relative whispered in my ear, "She was the one I was messing with when the Crips surrounded the house."

"You had sex with her yet?" I asked.

"No," he said. "She's a virgin."

I wanted to get to her then. Not only was she a cross-town, but she was a rival's sister. The bulge in my pants stood at attention.

The night started off slow, and I was trying to put a smile on her face and get close to her. It took some time to get them into the house. It took even longer to get her to the bedroom. I snuggled up on her and began whispering in her ear, and by the end of the night, I got her number. Immediately, I started calling her, whispering sweet nothings into her beautiful ear. She acted as if she weren't a Crip. I knew better and was careful not to ask her about her brother.

Soon after meeting her, I started going over to her house. She stayed in the heart of West Coast Crip hood. I had no respect for no Crip turf in San Diego, so going to her house would be fun, and I could do some recon.

It got intense fast the first time they found out I was inside the home. Luckily, she had a security door that was not easily penetrated. They would come over to her house quickly because she was a fine homegirl, and she kept home girls over there who were just as fine.

One night, they showed up looking for her. I came to the door, taking my stuff. Immediately, they asked who I was and where I was from. I banged on them. It got intense real fast, and they wanted in or for me to come out. But because the family was well respected and loved, they would only bang so much. This was helpful info for me. After showing me they had cannons, the situation went up a notch. I still acted like it wasn't nothing and they made the call.

Next thing you know, the house was surrounded by Crips. I went to the back of the house, and there they were. Went to a bedroom window, and there they were, talking trash. I started laughing and then flashed my gang sign. I had my gun on me and wasn't tripping off them.

I began watching television, and her mom came home from the motorcycle club. She walked into the room, looked at me, and said, "If you're scared, I got a gun for you if you want to feel straight while chilling with Lovely." She looked like an older version of Lovely, a beautiful sight. I could tell she was buzzing. I pulled out my gun and said, "I'm good, but thanks." Usually, I wouldn't do that, but I wanted mom and daughter to know who I was and who they were dealing with. Her mom smirked but didn't say anything. At that moment, I fell in love with her family, which did nothing but encourage me to come more often. I would go through their neighbourhood disrespecting their turf and being a crash dummy, but I didn't care. I wanted to get in between those creamy thighs, and if showing out would help, I would do it.

I pulled up in a shiny red '72 two-door Impala bumping "Piru Love" from the *Banging on Wax* album turned up to the max. Just as soon as I hit the corner, it was her and all her friends— ten or more. Immediately, I pulled to the side, hopped out, and started talking to her. After a few minutes, I returned to the car and burnt rubber. I left the same way I came this time, knowing I wasn't supposed to. The shots rang out as soon as I flew past their neighbourhood hangout. They didn't hit anything but told me they were on to me.

I got my license and quickly got a cheap throwaway car. It was registered to a foreigner who didn't know me, and I didn't know them. Perfectly suitable for us to begin a war path. Gino "Lunatick" Langston would also use the car since I didn't want us going to jail for stealing one. Gino was an early teenager then, and my family didn't like it because he was too young to drive—as if he hadn't taught me how to drive a stick shift when I was ten. The throwaway car was a stick shift; he could probably drive it better than me.

Every time I was in that car, I was doing the most. I didn't care what it was. It could be running out to a store for liquor, food, and clothes. I could be driving down the street, and if a dude had on the wrong colour, I would try to run him down.

As soon as the sun set, the homie Too-Tall pulled up with a couple of homies in an old beat-up Cadillac. The homies knew we had the straps, and we loved to use them.

Too-Tall pulled me aside and said, "A hood rat told me that the Crips would be hanging later." Too-Tall messed with a lot of girls, so I valued his intel. "You want in?"

I looked him in the eye without saying a word.

While waiting for it to get dark, we made a couple of store runs, sipping on drinks and feeling the vibe. I didn't know the dudes he was with then but didn't care much to meet and greet. They were his people. Trigger Happy, and I got into our vehicle and followed them to the destination. Too-Tall pulled into the apartments. On the way there, we drove past them, and I saw them hanging deep. Given how deep they were, I figured that was what he talked about.

We all got out, and everybody started to check their guns and ensure they were ready to go before we gathered in a circle. Trigger Happy wasn't present because he went to take a piss.

Too-Tall whispered, "We going to walk on the trolley tracks just as soon as the trolley goes by."

We started walking on the tracks toward where they were hanging, creeping like a lion on a gazelle. Not only did we have the cover of darkness on our side, but the way it was set up, they couldn't see us until it was too late. One way in and one way out. Attempting to go inside would be catastrophic for us, so this was a perfect way to get to them while they were slipping and fading. You could tell they were posted and feeling comfortable: loud music, slurring, having a good time.

As we were in position, we heard Trigger Happy running loudly on the rocks next to the trolley tracks to catch up. None of us could say anything without drawing attention to ourselves. The lookout Crips yelled, "Dudes is on the tracks, cuz!"

We started blasting, and they started shooting back. We didn't have any cover except bushes. This lasted for about a second or two. Once we heard the bullets zipping past us, we ran back to our vehicles while shooting. I got to my car, Trigger Happy climbed in the passenger, and we got out of there. Instead of making a right when I came out, I went left up the hill until I got to the freeway and back to safety, talking to myself the entire way and hating Trigger Happy for blowing up the spot. From this point on, there would be no more group riding. It never worked out right for me.

The next day, my father burst into my bedroom and told me Uncle Lee had a spot we could take over. It was some duplexes in East San Diego, not far from the freeway. I always liked anything near a freeway since it meant a leisurely getaway.

As soon as we arrived, we looked over the spot inside and outside, checking the scene and feeling the situation out. There were no dudes other than Uncle Lee. About five strawberry hoes were running around. Some were around my dad's age, and some were my age, but by their bodies, I could tell they just got turned out.

Before I could have a seat, my dad said, "These strawberries are the cops," in an urgent whisper. "We're getting out of here!"

"What do you mean?" I asked. "We haven't done a sale yet. Why would they run up here on us?"

He looked at me and said, "It doesn't feel right. We are getting out of here right now!"

There was nothing I could say or do to deter him. I trailed him to the car.

Uncle Lee looked confused and asked, "Where are you all going?"

My father didn't say a word, and neither did I, trailing behind my dad in a double step. We hopped in the car and quickly made our way to the freeway. I was driving because my dad was already drunk at four in the afternoon. Just as soon as we hit the corner, an undercover surrounded us. When we got on the freeway, they pulled off, and another marked car jumped on us.

The entire time, my dad was saying, "You see them? You thought I was tripping. Look, you see them hopping on and off us. Please pay attention, it won't cost you anything. Don't act like you don't see them."

I said, "Yeah, Pop, I see them."

"I told you I wasn't tripping because I'm high on dope," he said. "Always follow your first mind." He was trying hard to drive his point into me and kept going. "Where is your dope? You got it tucked?"

"Yeah, Pop," I said while looking in my mirrors, watching the black and white that was trying to act like it wasn't trailing us.

We got off the freeway on Imperial Ave. I was trying to move as fast as possible through traffic without violating laws while Pops was lying back, allowing me to watch the mirrors since I was driving.

He asked, "Are they still back there?"

"Yeah."

"I told you I will be feeling it," he said. "That's why you must always go with your gut, son. Forget Uncle Lee, forget those strawberry girls."

Now we were in Encanto, still swerving through traffic, and every time I looked back, they were not far behind. Why were they still following us? Why wouldn't they pull us over? I didn't want to take them to our home so that they could run up in it later.

"Dad, you want me to go home?" I asked.

He said, "Yeah, forget them."

"You think Uncle Lee got them on us?"

"I wouldn't doubt it," he said, continuing with the usual, "you know you can't trust nobody in this game."

As soon as we got to our house and pulled into the driveway, the police stopped short on a corner nearby, made a U-turn, and left without incident. I had to admit that was very peculiar. Of course, my dad immediately asked me for a bump. After that spooky situation, I didn't mind.

Lemon Grove is a city on the outskirts of my turf, considered by many to be neutral. One day, I noticed two enemies in a big box truck U-Haul on a long stretch of road with no stop signs or lights. It was an ideal spot to blast them and keep them moving. My mind began racing, overjoyed with the possibility of catching some cross-towns on this perfect day. Anytime you don't have to go too far from the turf, it is almost an automatic getaway; most consider it a free kill.

Then I looked over at the homie and thought to myself, *Damn, I'm with this guy, the wrong person for this*. My mind was fighting me, going back and forth. I couldn't allow this beautiful opportunity to be wasted, so I told this dude he would have to be involved cause I couldn't let this blessing slip away. He was shaking, afraid of what would happen if he didn't cooperate, but I completely ignored his feelings.

I whispered, "Blood, I need you to catch up and pass them up. Get in front of them so I can come out the window and give it to them."

"Are you sure?" he asked.

Defiantly, I said, "Yes. Now press on the gas and pass them up so I can handle my business."

He pressed on the gas, but not enough to pass them. Instead, he exposed us. Suddenly, they looked down on us, identifying us and our intentions.

"Come on, man, go!" I said. "Go! Drive this piece of crap!" I pulled the burner out and turned to start blasting. As soon as I got off a shot, the U-Haul swerved into this little bucket, ran off the road into the centre divider, and then back across the entire street, ending on the trolley tracks. The U-Haul kept rolling until it was out of sight.

I screamed at the top of my lungs, "Damn!" I looked at his car and then him and said, "Forget this piece of crap car."

That was how it went whenever I hung out with him while I was trying to put in some work. It wasn't his fault, and I never considered how he felt about anything. That was selfish on my part. He was no gangster, more like a player/comedian.

After getting my blood pressure up, I called Hoe Bear, hoping she could bring me back to earth with a good nut. She picked up and began talking about some girls in her apartments looking to date.

"That's cool for later," I said, "but get your butt over here for now."

She was waiting for me before I could get back from the store. Immediately, we went to my bedroom. I popped the top on my Thunderbird and poured in the cherry Kool-Aid while she fired up a cigarette, hit it, and put it into my mouth. I took a good gulp, and she took it away. Then she led me to the bed.

I lay on my stomach while she put on some music. She put some lotion on my back and began giving me a massage, rubbing my shoulders, neck, and temples in a circular motion. I took a long drag of the cigarette before she pulled it from my lips and put it in the ashtray. She rubbed more lotion on her hands, massaged my entire body, turned me over, and started from the top of my head to my toes. My penis was on rock status. She put her head on top of my penis and began doing it how I loved it, looking deep into my eyes, whispering, "I can see you stressed, Daddy. Give that energy to me, baby. Let it off, Daddy." She cupped my balls in her hands while spitting on my shaft, and as soon as I closed my eyes to enjoy almost coming into her hands, she stopped.

I opened my eyes, and she was climbing on top. She began jumping up and down, saying, "Give me that energy, gangsta. I got you, baby." She went harder and harder, faster and faster. I grabbed her ass and began giving her some bite back, banging deep inside her with every stroke. She could tell I was ready to explode, then hopped off just as fast as she straddled me. Looking back at me, she got in doggy style with her head low on the pillow and an arch in her back.

She put my shaft inside and said, "Beat it up, Daddy, release all that stress, baby."

I did more than she asked for. She began shaking from her head to her toes, coming rushing down my balls—it felt like she was peeing on me. That made me go harder, faster. She pulled it out quickly and put it inside her butt. Instantly, it felt hot, tight, and unforgettable.

She said, "Go hard, Daddy. You shouldn't be stressed with bad energy."

With the music bumping, I attempted to dig a ditch in every hole in her body.

"Give it to me, baby!" She tried to hold onto her screams as I spread her butt cheeks apart. With her head against the wall with a pillow taking off the edge, I banged hard with each stroke.

"Pull it out, Daddy, and shove it in my tight twat."

I did as she asked, and instantly, she was gushing all over me and the bed. I couldn't hold out any more and busted like never before, letting out a loud yell. I was utterly oblivious to anyone inside the home.

She looked at me and said, "Do you feel better, baby?" as she fired up another cigarette and handed it to me. I was speechless.

At this time, CK Bill was staying with a girl from the rival set, and, in my eyes, she was a possible threat. She acted as if she was sparked, calling herself "Mrs. Billy 'CK Bill' Matthis." I knew her from junior high school and thought she might not have known who I was because she was a grade above me.

I told CK Bill, "Gangster, don't tell that broad what my name is, on Piru."

The difference between CK Bill and me is that he wanted the enemies to know everything about his doings and dealings, and I didn't want anybody to know anything about me—not even my homies from the turf. However, I now knew one of the two was impossible to achieve.

By this time, she gave us valuable intel on her folks, the ones we were attempting to down. The enemy knew he lived over there because of her; she was just as loud as he was in the scheme of things and wanted everybody in the world to know she was with him since CK Bill was one of the hottest dudes in Southeast San Diego. I saw it as a bad situation that could worsen, so I couldn't tell him anything, even though he was my big homie.

I found myself creeping through there regularly and sometimes spending the night. CK Bill was like me and my family; he would have guns everywhere. In the cookie jar on top of the counter, in the washing detergent underneath the sink, in a Doritos bag in the cupboard, underneath the couch, under the couch cushion, in the bedroom, inside some shirt hanging on the hanger.

I said, "Damn fool, you ready for an ambush for real."

He looked at me with an evil mug and said, "You never know."

"Well, you should be paranoid messing with this cross-town broad like she the main thang."

Quickly, he said, "Naw, that's my wife."

I laughed and thought to myself, *He's crazy.*

"Well, for me, you know what my name is."

He said, "What?"

"Anything but my name," I said, then laughed. I was Billy Bob Thorton, for all I cared. I had nothing bad to say, but I wasn't humping on her. I did know an older homie from the rival hood who was in love with her.

Despite my mentor's efforts, I kept hanging and banging with CK Bill. I did, however, understand where my mentor was coming from. My style was just like the style of my mentor, but I was attracted to CK Bill and his will to rid the world of our enemies.

Later that night, we went on a mission. He got one of the homies who stole professional-type vehicles. We went to Peter Pan St. in my neighbourhood to pick it up. I looked it over and said to myself, *Damn, this car is beautiful.*

First stop: our rival's park. We left just after dark. We liked to go to at least two rival hoods in one night. Our thinking was that while they send officers to one location, we would be at another location where their efforts would be stretched thin.

As soon as we pulled into the park and stopped, shots began tearing our car apart. *Pow!* The windshield got shot out. CK Bill began firing an automatic. We hopped out of the car, got behind, and shot back. But it was dark, and they had the cover of a bathroom building, so we were wasting bullets and time. They stopped shooting, and we slid back into the car, backed out, and skirted to the freeway, going as fast as the wheels would take us. We went one way on the highway, then jumped back off and went in a different direction, watching our mirrors to see if there were any tails.

We got to a neutral area and decided to take a look at the vehicle, still hoping we could get to another turf, but there was too much damage to do anything except shake the car. We drove it as close as possible to our safe spot before shaking it like wet dogs. We ran, jogged, and walked 5 miles to safety, jumping fences and running through canyons to ensure we weren't followed. CK Bill was always ahead while I stayed close enough not to get left behind. This was how we did it anytime we moved around.

We both had agreed that we needed more firepower on the turf, so we had conjured up schemes. We started looking into security guards. Many businesses thought it best to get armed security guards, so they started popping up everywhere around the city. We saw this as an easy way to get guns.

We went all over the city looking for lazy armed guards with pistols on their waists. One would draw down, and the other would snatch their entire belt, stealing the guns. We would always search them like police officers, from the top of their heads to their shoes, hoping we didn't miss anything, then vanish into the night just as we appeared.

We felt the first one would be too easy. This guard was policing a 24-hour restaurant, sitting on a couch chair, almost falling asleep. We parked around the corner, then came the long way to pop up on him. By the time he noticed us, I had the pistol pointed at his face.

He opened his eyes, and CK Bill said, "We don't want nothing but your guns. We don't want your money. You can use that to buy another pistol so we can use yours." He giggled while checking the guard for weapons. He only had one. We took that and were gone just as fast as we came.

Chapter 9

'The High Speed'

The next day, CK Bill called me upset and irritated. He said, "Bro, you won't believe who came to the set. We had him right here at the park and didn't kill him."

I asked, "Who?"

"Woopty Woop, and what's his name." Those were two of the guys we'd been looking for. We'd even been in a couple of shootouts with them. "Our big homie told them to come up to our turf on some drug deal and thought it was ok," he continued. "I don't know who the big homie thought he was, but he learned who he's not the hard way.

"Then C.K. Bill begins explaining what happened. Then he told me the story. I was passing their car, and they looked out of place. I banged on them, and they gave up the rival turf. Immediately, I was all over them, pulling them out of their car. I looked up, and there was this young dude I never saw before helping me. Afterwards, we chased them out of the park, and they left their car. After the incident, the young homies told me that it was Woopty Woop and what's his name. Of course, you know how mad I was, not only at the OG but also at the young homies. While I was driving down the street and he was telling me the story, we saw the little homie he had been talking about who helped him. I pulled up on him. C.K. Bill hopped out and told him to hop in. We gave him a burner when he hopped into the back seat. Then, we immediately went across town to see what we could get into. After several hours with no luck, we returned to our turf."

The next night, CK Bill called me. "Pull up to your mentor's, bro. We have a lick to get later."

"I'm on my way."

When I arrived, my elders were ready to go on a mission across town. Not two minutes later, the homie pulled up in his car. We piled into his two-door Impala. CK Bill started rapping as soon as we got into the back seat.

I looked at him and said, "Come on with the stuff, bro. You know you can't rap." Everybody chimed in with jokes, and we all started laughing. We were flying down Imperial Ave. We kept the music low; the car was heavily loaded and didn't need any unwanted attention. We got near some apartments. The driver pulled to the sidewalk, and everyone but him hopped out. We were four deep. My mentor and Young Bugs went one way, and Ck-Bill and I went another.

When we thought we saw an enemy and were about to pull up, a guy walked out of the apartment. We didn't have anything over our faces.

"What's up, Blood?" he said, looking at me and the homie, catching us off guard.

CK Bill said, "What's up, Blood? Where are you from?" We both hoped he said a neighbourhood we were looking for, but he didn't. We both said we were from the same community and gave anything that came to mind. Then, we hurriedly left, hoping not to be there long enough to be able to provide a positive ID.

We found out it was no good when we returned to our safe house. We were lucky nothing happened. Then, two minutes later, the police hit the corner and flashed their lights on us. We were in the cut, where the police should not be looking for us unless we gave them our whereabouts. We all took off in different directions.

An hour later, thankfully, we all made it back to our neighbourhood. We huddled and agreed that it was shady business.

When CK Bill called me again the next night, I was ready for him with my crap. I said, "Blood, I'm not riding tonight. I'm hustling. I'll catch up with you in a few days."

He said, "Yo, you need a couple of dollars?"

"Yes."

"I'll call you in a couple minutes," he said. "Blood, pick up when I call."

I said, "Gotcha." But he must have known I was tired of his bullshit because he repeated it before he hung up.

When he called back, he said, "Blood, I'm about to pull up."

As soon as he pulled up, he hopped out, threw me a couple of dollars, and said, "Is that enough for the night?"

I counted it and said, "Ok, let's get it."

We jumped in my car and went across town to see what we could get into. This time, we had another homie that I never rolled with. However, the dude was, to my knowledge, a solid homie. We all grew up with each other.

As I parked, the car cut off, and he said, "Blood, I'm good."

"Blood, you good," I said, "I just let off the clutch too much. We good."

Then he started saying police stuff, like, "That looks like the police over there." Things like that shock waves the entire mission.

I looked at CK Bill like *Bro, this shit is no good.* He gave me the same look back. We left. I was glad he broke mine off with money because this would make me angry.

I was still on parole, but because I'd been out for so long, hadn't had any dirty drug test thus far, and graduated from high school, they'd become very lenient on me. I didn't have to check in as often and only had to take drug tests periodically.

My parole officer was a short, older Mexican female. She was obese. To me, she was more than obese. At this time, I could have sex with a lot of women, but I couldn't find anything about her that could get my penis hard. The last couple of times, she made an attempt on me sexually. The first time she had inquired about my sex life. I acted like I missed the hint. This time, she opened her drawer, reached into it, and took out a brown bag. She dug in and pulled out a handful of Trojan condoms of all colors and styles.

She looked me in the eyes and asked, "Are you having safe sex?"

I said, "Yes, ma'am."

She opened another drawer and brought out another bag. She put the handful of condoms inside and passed the bag to me.

"That looks like it might be enough to hold me," I said, smiling. "Thank you."

Then she held up some plastic square-shaped things, looked me in the eye again, and asked, "Do you know what these are?"

"No," I said.

She leaned in closer and, in a soft tone, almost a whisper, said, "Do you eat pussy?" I got shy and nodded my head up and down. "These are eating pussy condoms. Different flavours. When you suck and lick, it tastes like strawberries and grapes." She kept eye contact the whole time. Then she asked. "Do you know how to eat vaginas?"

I said, "I haven't had any complaints."

Then she added, "I'm going to have to show you how to use these, so I know you're safe." After seeing my look, she said, "Are you ready to take your piss test?"

I quickly agreed, then asked, "If somebody smoked around me, could that give me a dirty test?"

"Possibly," she said. "How much do you think they smoked around you?"

"Maybe a couple of ounces."

"Damn!" she exclaimed. "That must be some backyard boogie. It can't be no good."

I acted dumb. "Backyard boogie? Good?"

She said, "It can't be good if they smoke that much around you."

I said, "I don't know."

"Well, I'm not going to test you this time, but don't be around anyone while they are smoking, because next time, I'll be testing you." Then she added, "You can leave."

I pondered if she was making moves on me. I hoped she wasn't because I wouldn't know what to do. There were only a couple of plays that I could make. I could allow it to go to the next level and see where it goes with the possibility of getting off parole sooner rather than later. But I figured if I did that, I could also become something like a slave to her. She didn't have anything to offer sexually. Her obesity was too much for me to bear; the way her fat hung down on the side of her pants looked like huge balls to me. She had a bunch of moles on her face that made it hard for me to look at her. Simply put, she wasn't attractive to me anywhere. At this stage in my life, I could usually find anything: pretty feet, a nice smile, cute nails, but with her, there was absolutely nothing.

The next time I went to see her, she sat me down and asked if I was ready to give a urine sample.

"Yes, always," I said.

"Did you use the condoms I gave you?" she asked. "And more importantly, did you use the oral ones?"

I quickly said yes, wanting to sound like I was a safe-sex type of guy.

"Do they taste fruity?" she asked. I thought it was a trick question.

"Fruity enough," I answered. "It takes away the acquired taste."

"Do you still have condoms left?" she asked, knowing she gave me enough to last months. I told her they were gone, and she got a nasty look on her face like she was cumming in her seat. She began moving from side to side like she had ants in her pants.

In almost a whisper, she said, "That was a lot of condoms."

I said, "Yes, there were, and many of them broke because I'm too big." She got quiet. "I said I would put ten on the bed. Almost all of them would brake by the time I climaxed." She looked like her top was about to pop. I couldn't respond; I was frozen like a possum in headlights.

Then she said, "Don't trip the urine sample this time. Would you like some more condoms?"

"Yes," I said, "if you have a bigger size than your average." I could tell everything I said was making her mind wander with passion.

"Do you have some oral condoms left?" she asked.

"I'm eating away with those things."

"I will be getting in touch with you to see if you are using the condoms as directed," she said.

Later that day, at my grandma's house, I was trying to figure out how I would be able to deal with this situation. Speaking with my dad, he said, "Flat out suck on her twat and get off parole ASAP. Don't be a sucker. Handle your business and take one for the team. What is the worst that could happen?"

"She could dangle getting off parole in front of me forever and make me bow to her will," I said. The only thing I saw coming from this was a violation of parole if I didn't act accordingly, unless I found a way to prove we had been sexing. What would she do if I stopped wanting to bow and have sex with her? It scared me to think about it. She wasn't okay; she was not going to get another man, probably ever, and would use any means she wanted to hang on to me like grim death.

He laughed and said, "You're just being a girl. You're way overthinking this, son." Unlike him, I thought I knew best about my sex game. The bottom line is that he wasn't seeing what I saw, so talking with him was going nowhere. I had to figure this out myself.

Usually, I would just have sex with her, but this time, I had to change it up because she had too much power over me. I decided that I would change parole officers if I could. I didn't care who they would assign me to. I had been on for some time that my level dropped, and they were dealing with me differently.

I called the supervising officer. I told him that my parole officer and I weren't on the same page and, if it were possible, I would like another. He obliged and changed parole officers the next week.

The next officer I got was a black woman with a caramel complexion and a real hardball. She had short hair, like a lesbian, and a bad attitude. It was how she acted, almost like she didn't like men, period. Immediately, I didn't want her, and she didn't like me. She gave me a bottle to piss in the first time we met. I was still not smoking, so I didn't care. I told her I was looking for work and to hook me up with the job specialist they had down there cause I wanted a job. After the test came back clean, she eased up and off me a bit.

My childhood love and I never could consummate our relationship, mostly because I would always go to jail. Before that, it would always fizzle out first. Her name was Destiny, and I always felt our relationship was destined for the long haul.

Destiny was a Crip, and I met her at my relative's birthday party when I was 12. At the party, she had on all blue: blue corduroy pants, a blue shirt, and, for some odd reason, a blue snakeskin belt around her neck. Immediately, I was smitten with this girl. She stayed way across town, so it was nearly impossible to see each other. We had to get to know each other through the phone, where we would talk about everything; I believe that was why I was so obsessed with her.

She was in a relationship with a military dude, and I was with Dimples. Dimples was a girl I had known since I was in the sixth grade; she was in the fifth. Dimples and I were from the same set. I watched her get jumped in by the home girls. After that, I got her to the 69 Motel, an abandoned house in the hood we would squat in. By squatting, I mean we would party, sleep, and post. This is where she gave in to me devirginizing her. Now she had a son by another dude. I liked her but felt she wasn't the one for the long haul—more for the moment. Dimples and I were sharing an apartment in Spring Valley. Because I wasn't feeling her, she and I would fight a lot. It was obvious she wasn't feeling me either. Still, we would make nice deals with each other. By this point, there was a lot of domestic violence on both our parts.

By the time I bumped into Destiny again, I was ready for a change. The fact that she had a man at this time wasn't making me look at her differently. She picked me up in her brand new ride; she said her dude made payments. They had an apartment in Casa De Oro, a part of Spring Valley. At the apartment she shared with her boyfriend, we had a drink and started watching porn. From the porn, she and I started spooning. This led us to the bedroom. I was overjoyed that I was finally getting to those panties. I knew she had a dude, and I didn't care; I was ready to taste her.

She lay down on the bed. She had a small frame, small tits with a nice butt, and chocolate skin. I kissed her from the top of her head to her feet, then spread her legs open and kissed around her lips before parting them open with my tongue. She gasped when I did this. Softly, I snuggled my mouth inside her sex box. I'd waited for this moment for years, and she tasted great. I wanted to absorb her love nest before moving on to sexing her. By the time I put the tip in, I was ready to bust. In my mind, I was in love with this girl. She felt so good to me, and not long after entering her, I split.

Immediately after having sex, her dude called. She answered while we were still lying on the bed, playing with my hair while talking to her man. I fell asleep, and she was still on the phone when I awoke. I remember thinking to myself, *Damn, she's good*.

Because her man was in the Navy, he often worked at the base. This allowed us more time to hang out during most days. She went down to the military people to try to enlist in the Air Force, and her friends tried to do so, too. This encouraged me to try; it might be the one shot I got to change and save me from doing life or getting killed. I tried to enlist, but I didn't even get past the part of questioning. I told them that I had asthma in my history, and after about two minutes, they said there wasn't a snowball's chance in hell of me joining any military field.

I said, "It doesn't affect me now and hasn't in a long time. I know there is some test I could try out for."

Still, they said no. I got shut down. This made me feel as though the life of a gangster was fate.

Back at her place, she set the mood right by lighting candles. This time, it was her turn to show me how much she had grown. She laid me down and kissed me from the top of my head to my feet, then back up to my penis. She teased, sucked, and licked, all while keeping eye contact. Then we got to some intense sex. I busted a nut deep into that love box, asking God to allow one of my seeds to make it to her egg.

Just as soon as we were done, her dude called to check-in. Something about him being hungry and wanting her to bring him something. While they were on the phone, I started watching TV. She started cooking and was on the phone the entire time. After about an hour on the phone, we got in the car and took him his food. The whole time we rolled, I was getting lost in my thoughts. First, I thought I was special. Then I thought she was too good at cheating, which would not be suitable for my mind. If I were him, I would not suspect anything. I would think that my lady was down and dedicated to the fullest.

After dropping off the plate, I told her to take me to my grandma's house.

When I got there, I washed up to get the scent of another woman off of me. Just as soon as I entered the apartment, Dimples was riding my ass about who I was with and who I was sexing. I told her she was tripping like always. Just as soon as I lay down, she acted like she was going to jack my penis off. Then she quickly pulled her hand out and, when she thought I wasn't looking, pretended like she was scratching her face and then moved her hand across her nose. I never saw that play before and started laughing. I was cracking up; she didn't care at all. This did lead to a fight. We were fighting so tough that she threw a glass table at me. Standing by the balcony with the door open, the glass hit the balcony and broke everywhere. It rained down on the people smoking below, and they all scattered like roaches. Thank God this was the part of town where nobody heard or saw anything.

Aunty Sis, who lived across from us, was the one putting everything in Dimples' head. Aunty Sis was good for stuff like this. She was a Gemini, so one day, she would be on my team, and the next, she would be on her team. It was ridiculous. I learned fast that I must play my aunty just as I played Dimples.

I went to my mother's house to get a break from Aunty Sis and Dimples. While there, my mother was interested in my love life.

She liked Dimples. She also liked Destiny. When I told her what was going on with Destiny, she quickly said, "Hm, that's not going to be good for the future of your relationship."

I asked, "How so?"

"She's good at the cheating game. That doesn't mess with your mind?"

She drove her point in deep, and I said, "Yes."

I was done with Destiny when I left to go home to Dimples.

Chapter 10

'Body Bag'

Me, Lunatick, and Trigger Happy were cleaning our weapons at the back of the house. None of us were talking; we were concentrating on thoroughly examining our weapons and the mission that we were about to get on.

I finally whispered, "Blood, all of you dudes must get on your mission. I don't need all of you messing up my kill tonight."

Lunatick chimed in and said, "Your kill? Tonight is my kill."

Trigger Happy laughed and said, "Relative, I messed up that last mission by mistake. Tonight, I can feel it in the air like Phil Collins. It's going to be my kill. Look me in the eyes and tell me you don't see the Devil. I'm the body snatcher."

Lunatick laughed eerily and said, "You couldn't hit a mark if he was two feet away."

"Y'all need to get on your mission because I'm getting my kill tonight," I said again, "and I don't need you two messing up destiny."

"Fool, you tripping," Lunatick said. "I got this. It's all good. Just let me know the play, and I will deliver like Domino's."

"Relative, stop tripping now," Trigger Happy said, rocking back and forth.

I said, "Alright, I'm feeling the energy," while Mac Mall's "Untouchable" played low in the background. "What y'all on?"

"What?" Lunatick asked. "I'm on murder, boy."

I said, "Drugs, fool? What have you all been smoking?" I took the cigarette out of my mouth and ashed it in the ashtray.

Trigger Happy said, "Fool, pass the BIG. That's the only thing I'm on."

We snuck out the bedroom window; we wanted our family to think we were still there in case of an alibi. One by one, we went over the fence as quietly as possible. Once we reached the front of the house, we looked back and listened. Nobody heard or saw us.

Around the corner, we had a car we had stolen earlier that day. I was driving, Lunatick was in the back, and Trigger Happy was in the passenger. Everybody in the car was quiet; the only sound came from the radio. C-Bo's "Straight Killer" was playing, which helped us settle into the mood.

"We are not going to no hood tonight," I said. We were going to known hangouts, driving on the backstreets hoping to avoid unwanted attention. "I don't want to hear no cop shit or y'all never riding with me again."

Lunatick said, "That be Trigger Happy with that bullshit," as we slid down the street.

"Go past the Pinkies," Trigger Happy said. "You know it be cross towns sliding in and out. You never know what we might see."

I thought about it and agreed. We hit a few corners and eased up to a parking spot I felt would be undetected. I turned off the lights and cut the engine. We waited.

I told Trigger Happy, "Your little broad often has enemies sliding through. This your bitch, this is your lick. These fools don't have enough names for me. I'm trying to knock me down a giant."

As soon as I said that, two dudes came out of the apartment, talking on the rails. I looked at Trigger Happy.

Lunatick said, "This fool is not about to do shit."

"Pull up, relative," Trigger Happy said.

I answered, "No. You'll have to sneak up and hit the dude and get back. We will be on the next street waiting for you." He looked at me like I was going to shake him. I added, "On the set."

Then Lunatick said, "Blood if you don't hit anything, don't slide up on us."

"Forget you, Blood," Trigger Happy said, quickly sliding out the whip.

I started the car and slid off as Trigger Happy jumped over a gate. When we hit the block and got to the meeting spot, I heard shots fired and a car zooming down the street in a panic. The car kept going.

"I told you he wasn't going to hit nothing. His CK stands for cloud killer," Lunatick said, laughing like an evil dude in a scary movie. "Come on, big bro, let's leave this fool and get on our mission."

I thought about it and said, "Don't trip. We'll drop him off at the spot and get on our mission." As soon as the words left my lips, Trigger Happy jumped into the car.

I asked, "What happened with the walk-up?"

"Blood. By the time I got there, they were already in the car and leaving," Trigger Happy answered. "I didn't want to get spotted, so I waited for them to come out before firing." Lunatick laughed. "Now I'm out of bullets," Trigger Happy finished.

"Alright then, we going to take you to the spot," I told him. I pulled off slowly, careful to switch on my blinkers before turning the corner.

Five minutes later, we dropped off Trigger Happy. He was still out of breath, chest pumping, adrenaline flowing.

"Fool, you didn't hit nothing," Lunatick said. "Damn sure didn't kill nothing. You look like you are feeling good about the work you did today. You fired."

Trigger Happy turned to look at Lunatick and said, "F you, fool. I'll be watching the news to see what you do."

I pulled the car to the curb two blocks from the spot and said, "Alright, reli, we'll be back to get you when it's over." Trigger Happy jumped out of the car and left. Lunatick climbed up front.

As soon as he jumped into the front seat, he said, "Alright, let's get it on."

We drove every back street until we got to a popular hangout. I pulled over to a location I felt was incognito, cut off the lights, turned the car off, and leaned the seats back.

I lit a cigarette and said, "Listen, just as soon as I notice a dude with a name, I'm going to take the long way, and you take the short way. We are going to meet at the dude and light his ass up like a Christmas tree. Whoever gets there first, handle your business because I will handle mine. We can't mess this up. We must get the kill if it's more than one; that makes it better. You got me?"

He whispered, "Yes," while Tupac's "Soldier's Story" played in the background on low.

After smoking a couple of cigarettes, I spotted someone I felt would hurt a little bit. I said to Lunatick, "You see him right there? Yeah, the one that has on this and that. He just came out eating a sandwich."

He said, "Yes."

"That's the target," I said. "Listen, I'm about to go the long way. Give me an extra minute or two. Don't linger. If you get the shot, take it. You hear me?"

He agreed.

I looked in the mirrors before exiting the vehicle and carefully climbed out. I went over a fence and then crept through an apartment complex. It was dark now, and the cover of darkness assisted me as I crept through the front gate and an alleyway to get to the main street.

After what seemed like forever, I saw the enemy as I peeked around a bush. I pulled out my pistol and checked it one last time, making sure the safety wasn't on, and held it at my side as I came out on the main street. Just as soon as I hit the main street, I saw Lunatick. We crossed the road at the same time. Even though I was moving in stealth mode, I knew I would get to the enemy first. Lunatick's little legs couldn't keep up with mine; he would have to watch me get the K.

The enemy finished his food and was on his way to his car. When he pulled out his keys, I was there instantly. I fired the first shot. He hit the ground, eyes wide like he wanted to run, but his legs wouldn't move. I stood over him. He put his arms over his face as I let loose over his upper torso. Then, just as quickly as I came, I left.

Lunatick was still coming. I looked at him as if to say, *He's dead. Let's roll.* With the clip gone and the body lying still, he changed directions and was gone.

I crossed the street, careful not to go the same way I came. I entered another alley and quickly cut through another apartment complex unseen. Just as soon as I hit a fence to a backyard, I heard the sirens. This made me move faster. I took a long way back to the car just in case someone had noticed me. My relative lived nearby, so I knew my route. No dogs, no lights.

After what seemed like forever, I made it back to the car. Lunatick was sunk low in the car when I jumped in. He was excited for me, but we were both quiet. I fired up a cigarette.

He said, "Blood, come on, let's roll."

"Hold up," I said, "and listen." We both looked around before I quietly asked, "Do you see anyone?"

Lunatick whispered, "No," as I passed him the cigarette, started the car, and crept to the street. An ambulance and cops were going to the location, so we went in the opposite direction. After a light or two, we entered the freeway, going this way and that before heading to where we dropped Trigger Happy off. We both looked toward the festivities.

Just as soon as we arrived, the news was on, the excitement on full display. Trigger Happy already told people what Lunatick and I were on, though we were careful not to claim responsibility.

After smoking a cigarette with my uncle, I asked Trigger Happy, "You ready?" I had no interest in watching the havoc I created on the news. Everyone else watched Lunatick and me as if they knew it was our work. They were guessing, and I knew we should get out of there as fast as possible.

We climbed into the car and drove home, parking in another location. Then we removed the ashtray, wiped it down thoroughly, and returned to our house, carefully getting to our bedroom the same way we left. We all removed our clothes and put them into the grill, threw some lighter fluid on them, lit it, and closed the lid.

My aunt knocked on the door when we were safely in the room.

"Are y'all in there?"

"Yes," I answered.

"You had a phone call," she said.

"Tell them to call me back."

When we had all put on new clothes, I opened the door.

I walked into my grandmother's room to shower, and as I did, my grandmother was listening to the police scanner while eyeing me down intently. I continued towards the bathroom. My aunt walked into the bedroom and asked Grandma if she was barbecuing.

With my back to both of them, I shut the door.

While I was in the shower, a car pulled up. I listened. Four car doors slammed shut. Then I heard my other aunt describing how the entire street was on lockdown and that they had police looking for suspicious vehicles and didn't make it to the dope spot because of it. I smiled.

When I got out of the shower, my two aunts and grandmother were eyeing me down. I didn't say anything. As soon as I got to the bedroom, my father busted in.

"Give me the gun, son!" he said, sweating profusely.

I said, "What gun?"

"What y'all barbecuing?" he asked, eyeing me and Lunatick suspiciously. I looked right back at him. "Can I have some?" he asked, but I said nothing. Then he started talking about cops being everywhere and how they would be here soon.

"We were here all night," I said.

"We all know y'all did it!" he said. "You shot somebody."

Lunatick laughed out loud. I stared at my father, then said, "We did nothing."

"Give me the gun so I can get rid of it before they get here," he continued. "More importantly, so you don't go to jail."

I looked him in the eye and said, slow "I... Don't... Have... Nothing..." He must have been spooked because he turned around and left without saying another word.

Lunatick and I went to check on the barbecue. The entire house was dead silent as we walked through the living room. We got to the backyard, and the clothes were almost all ash. I lit a cigarette and blew it out.

Lunatick said, "We are good."

Then I said, "I got to go and get my K, bro." I just stared into the sky. "Come on, let's get dressed and get out of here. The family is tripping hard." He agreed. "Change your shoes first, and hide the ones we wore in Uncle's room. He wears the same size."

When we were finished, we drove to the hangout. As soon as we entered, everyone was eyeing us.

"We got to get out of here," I whispered to Lunatick. "They are making me nervous." He agreed that they were eyeing us. When I made eye contact, they would turn their heads fast. What were they so nervous about? I wondered why everyone thought that they knew it was us who went to work.

"Where are you going?" asked Lunatick. I said I need some sex badly. You know how I get when I get off work.

"I'm going to stay and soak up the energy," he said. "I'll tell you what everyone's thinking tomorrow." He laughed eerily and said, "Big bro, you're just paranoid."

I nodded and left.

Chapter 11

'The Rules'

Early one afternoon in Spring Valley, I was walking through the gate of my relative Nutso's apartment complex when an enemy of mine and I caught eye contact. I thought he would still be on bed rest since he had just been shot up and nearly died not too long before. When I saw him, I thought I saw a ghost. I was highly disappointed by him surviving the ordeal.

I mean, mugged him. Then I said, "What is Skyline Piru like?"

He said, "What that Lincoln Park Bloods like?" Then he quickly added, "You know they call me PK?"

I said, "You know they call me BK?"

"What's happening then?"

"Whatever you want to be happening."

We squared up to fight on the sidewalk on a busy street before I said, "Hold up. We can't get in a good fight here."

"You right," he said.

I returned to my homeboy Nutso's apartment and gave him my burner. Nutso asked what was up, and I smiled.

He and I were back outside in an instant.

Me and this dude first met one another in junior high school. On the first day of school, he walked up with his crew and banged on me. I banged back. From that day on, we mugged one another. His homeboy Ra'son "Baby-Wood" Evans was the leader of the crew. He and I started being cool, so he had to be cool with it.

Then he got put up a grade and started going to high school. One day, I came out of school, and he got there just as we did. He jumped off his bike, took his gloves out of his back pocket, looked at me with a mean mug, and said, "What is Lincoln Park like?"

Without a second thought, I fired at his jaw. It was so loud the entire school turned their heads to see what happened. He dropped the bike. I squared up. Then, the school surrounded us.

Just when he was about to say green light, Baby Wood said, "No green light!" That was a G call, meaning he and I could get the head up fade, and his homeboys wouldn't jump me.

Now that I could relax without thinking I would get jumped, I gave him the business. Since that day, we have become enemies.

I said, "Come on, I know we can find somewhere to get down."

We walked around the neighbourhood looking for somewhere to fight without going to jail for getting our scrap on. After not finding anything close by, he mentioned that he had an empty bedroom that we could get down at. I didn't give two shits about where; I just wanted to beat that ass, and inside a vacant apartment sounded good to me.

First, I stopped at my people's house next door to tell them what was happening. Then he went in to let his girlfriend know what was happening and get it situated for the fade. When we were walking around to find a place to fight, he said he was trying to find some grass so we could roll around.

I said, "I'm not wrestling." I should have known then that was what he was trying to do. I looked him in the eyes and said, "Look here: it's just you and I. Your homies are not here, and mine's not here. If you hit the ground, I'm going to let you get up, and if I hit the ground, you let me get up."

He agreed.

When we walked into his apartment, the living room was straight ahead. The room we were fighting in was to the left, and his girlfriend, my home girl, was in the back room to the right. I walked into the room, and he returned with some juice boxes. He gave me one and kept one.

Then he asked, "How's your family doing?"

I said, "Forget them, let's get down." I never even tripped off the windows not being opened.

We squared up. He came in, and I gave him a two-piece and damn near knocked him out. I backed up and let him regain his composure. As soon as he did, he rushed in, and I gave him another two-piece, but he got a hold of me, and then the wrestling match began.

I say, "Piru, get off me and shoot the heads. Get off of me, Blood!"

Of course, he wasn't listening because that was what he wanted to do from the get-go. I just thought the fool had some solidarity about his gangsterism; it was silly of me to believe that he wouldn't get down like that. However, where I just came from while incarcerated, that was typical behaviour.

We were on the ground, and I wasted all my energy on not letting him get the best of me. It was then the heat of Spring Valley started to make an impact. I noticed the windows were not open, and then I started panicking. After a few more minutes of this, I would be a goner because my asthma would quickly begin to affect me.

His nuts were right there, so with one swift move, I swung and hit him good, then jumped up and got the fuck out of there.

That night, I staked him out for hours, hoping he would move. I did see him peeking out of the windows every couple of minutes. I knew he felt me all around him. He and I had been rivals for a long time, and he knew he violated what he pulled. He never could scrap good, no way. I don't know what I thought by fighting him in his apartment. Truthfully, I wasn't thinking. I just wanted to beat him up cause I was angry he was still breathing.

I continued checking on him in the next few days to see if I could catch him slipping. I would also ask his neighbour to let me know his movements. I was still going to my people's house and didn't see him moving around as much anymore.

One of my neighbors was a dope fiend, and I gave her some dope on credit. It wasn't much. The trouble is she wasn't paying anything, not even a couple of dollars here and there. Then I heard from the other dope boys around the way that she was spending money with them—real money, not no credit.

The system I was brought up under was if you owe me a nickel, I need my nickel. Because of this, it mattered that she was running around spending instead of handling her debt with me. Although she lived next door, I couldn't find her because she was ducking me. I had my smoker aunt set it up so that I could get at her.

I didn't plan on what happened next.

I saw her go over there, and she didn't think I was anywhere around because she was hiding from me. I was on my way as soon as she slid into my aunt's apartment. I brought my homie's knife along since I intended to make her fear for her life.

As soon as I saw her, I asked, "Where is my money?"

She looked like she would play games about my money, so I slapped her across the face. Then, I pushed the knife in her direction, but not to kill or to cause bodily harm. When I pulled the knife back out, it had blood on the tip.

She got off of the couch, staggering out the door, holding her chest. I didn't think I did that much damage, especially since I wasn't trying. I just wanted to put some fear in the woman. Then I noticed drops of blood on the ground, trailing from the apartment, down the steps, and around the corner. I thought I might have messed up more than I had hoped. Then I heard ambulances coming and flashing lights. I had to get out of there. As soon as I started to panic, my boy Fidgety pulled up. I hopped in the car and said, "We got to get out of here like yesterday." He pulled out and drove towards the freeway.

He asked, "What happened?

"I just stabbed a smoker," I said. "I wasn't trying to mess her up, and I'm hoping she's exaggerating."

He said, "Yeah?"

"Hell yeah," I said. "Cause I sure wasn't trying to hurt the broad!"I just wanted to scare her. I was stressed out and couldn't think straight, so I said, "First, take me to my grandma's house so I can grab a few things."

When we were leaving my grandma's house, Fidgety ran into a car and did some real damage. Paranoid from what happened earlier, I backed away from the scene to hide in the cut. I knew the cops would come because of where the incident took place.

Just as soon as I thought about the police, there they were. I watched the scene play out from a distance. Then I noticed while the cops were talking with all parties from the accident, they began watching and pointing in my direction. Then, I saw the cops get on their walkie-talkie's and return to their vehicles.

This made me suspicious, and I started jumping fences and running in an attempt to get away. I heard the sound of their vehicles quickly approaching. I found somewhere I thought would be an excellent place to hide. I was sweating profusely and out of breath, wondering if they were seriously looking for me. I had to be tripping. The people in the other car didn't have time to see me backing away.

Then I heard the helicopter approaching and a dog barking in the distance. I came out of my hiding spot and started running again. Suddenly, a light shone on me from the air. The dog was getting louder, and then the light disappeared. I thought I could find a car to get under to escape, but just as I heard the sound of the dog on my heels, the entire scene lit up again.

The cops yelled, "Onaje Barbee, come from underneath the car, or we are going to let this dog eat your butt out!"

"Okay!" I shouted.

The cop said, "Real slow!" I slid out from under the car as slowly as I could. Cops were everywhere, guns out.

"Lay down flat on your stomach with your arms spread out! Don't move!"

The cops put my hands behind my back, lifted me, and started walking me to the car while reading me my rights.

They took me to the substation to get processed. I didn't ask any questions. I was too busy, lost in thought, wondering what just happened. Then came the would've, could've, and they should've. I messed up, but how bad I still didn't know. The police weren't saying anything, and I wasn't asking either.

I lay down inside my cell, handcuffed to the bench, trying to find a position to rest and get ready for what lay ahead. I was no longer a juvenile; this would be my first time in county jail. I hadn't heard many stories about the county jail and never asked any questions about it.

After what seemed to be half a day, it was time to transfer me to the county jail in downtown San Diego. While in the backseat of the cop car, I would always look out of the window at everything I might not see for a long time, admiring the freedom that I used to have and all the people just living their lives. That was the part that made me the most uncomfortable. Still, I was optimistic about what happened and how bad it might be.

I hit the holding tank with my mean mug on a hundred, looking for enemies or bullies, not knowing what to expect. It was a crowded room with one telephone for us all to use. I noticed everyone was using the phone, and it was free to make a call. I told the person using the phone that I was next. He shook his head.

Meanwhile, a dude with crack still on him began attempting to put it in his booty. I turned my head when he gave me a strange look. Then, the dude on the phone started yelling and slammed the receiver down.

I walked up and called my Dimples, and she answered. Immediately, I missed her, and I got choked up. Then I got myself together and said, "Hey, baby," in a low voice. "I'm locked up in the county jail."

She started crying. I couldn't stand it, so I put the phone down.

Then, a cop stepped into the room and said it was time to go. I picked up the phone and said, "I will call back as soon as possible."

The next room was the extreme searching. We stripped. They said, "Now run your fingers through your hair. Open your mouth, lift your tongue, bend over and cough, and lift your nuts." Then they gave us our clothes and a bedroll before we went to another room. They called us out one by one to tell us our charges and bail amount. When they called my name, I walked up to a booth. It was my home girl. I was like, "What the hell?"

She said, "I work here."

Then she told me the charges: Attempted Murder and Assault with a deadly weapon with the intent to commit murder. No bail, parole hold. Then they put the bracelet on my wrist, and the cop took me back to the cell.

TO BE CONTINUED